Carol Stream Public Library
616 Hiawatha Drive
Carol Stream, Illinois 60188

BLOOD ON
THE RIMROCK

Other books by Phil Dunlap:

The Death of Desert Belle
Call of the Gun
Fatal Revenge

BLOOD ON
THE RIMROCK

•

Phil Dunlap

AVALON BOOKS
NEW YORK

Published by Thomas Bouregy & Co., Inc.
160 Madison Avenue, New York, NY 10016

Library of Congress Cataloging-in-Publication Data

Dunlap, Phil.
  Blood on the rimrock / Phil Dunlap.
    p. cm.
  ISBN 978-0-8034-9880-8 (acid-free paper) 1. Peace officers—
West (U.S.)—Fiction. 2. Stagecoach robberies—Fiction. 3.
Murderers—Fiction. I. Title.

  PS3604.U548B58 2008
  813'.6—dc22

                                    2007031926

PRINTED IN THE UNITED STATES OF AMERICA
ON ACID-FREE PAPER
BY HADDON CRAFTSMEN, BLOOMSBURG, PENNSYLVANIA

F

To the strong women in my life:
Judy, Michelle, Sally, Susan, and Bailey.
To the many new friends who read my stories
and graciously asked for more. And especially to the
bookstores and libraries who give writers and
readers a place to get acquainted.

2/08

Chapter One

Deputy U.S. Marshal Piedmont Kelly tugged at the brim of his cavalry-style Stetson to shade his eyes as he tried to focus the army field glass he'd borrowed—and never returned—from the supply sergeant at Fort Huachuca. His gaze followed a swiftly moving swirl of dust rising from the desert floor and heading his direction. He'd seen indications earlier in the day that a single rider, about two miles back, seemed to be dogging him; having reached higher ground in the rock-strewn foothills of a mountain range, he was now finally ready to give up on his initial assumption that it might just be some cowboy out looking for strays. Whoever it was had clung to his trail like an old hound on the scent of a coon. But who in his right mind tracked a marshal? He looked around for a good spot to sit and wait for whoever was foolish enough to let himself be spotted in the first place.

1

Off to the west, the sun had started its slide behind the Picacho Mountains, and it was late enough that making camp seemed a natural thing to do after a long day in the saddle. He came upon a small clearing ringed with high boulders—an appropriate place to build a fire—with enough long, dry grass along one side to make a comfortable bed for him and provide a feast for his tired black gelding. After unsaddling and hobbling his horse, he quickly set to gathering wood to build a small cook fire. Then Kelly untied his bedroll, took off his gun belt, and laid it across his saddlebags. He poured some water from his canteen into a pot, added some coffee, and placed it on a rock next to the blaze. He pulled his Winchester from its scabbard and chambered a round. Then this tall, thin man with a bushy mustache and well-lined face, a face that had yet to reach thirty years of age, leaned back against his saddle, held the rifle close to his body, and pulled his blanket across his legs, hiding the Winchester from view.

And he waited.

The first hint that he was about to get a visit from his pursuer was the unnatural hush that suddenly fell over the darkening desert. No crickets singing their mating melodies, no fluttering night birds trying to settle down, no skittering sounds of small rodents darting about in search of an evening meal. Nothing but an almost eerie calm, an end to the normal sounds of life that had kept him company night after night on the trail. A slight rustling caught his ear. It came from just beyond a mesquite tree, where he spotted the shadowy form of a man, just barely visible. The man's gun was still in its holster, but he kept his hand close to it. Over his other arm he carried a bulging pair of saddlebags.

"Evenin', stranger," Kelly said. "C'mon in, sit, and share some coffee with me."

The man looked about nervously before stepping out of the shadows and into the light of the fire. He was scruffy, unshaven, and dirty. His youthful but troubled face spoke volumes about a life that had been hard and unkind. A scar across one cheek could have been an old knife wound, but Kelly wasn't about to get closer to find out.

"You all alone out here, mister?" the man said. His gaze fell to Kelly's gun belt lying about two feet away, out of reach unless a sudden lunge was made for it.

"Pretty much, except for you, of course," said Kelly. His vest completely covered his badge, so he doubted the man knew he was talking to the law.

The man's hand slowly moved toward his sidearm.

"You aimin' to draw that thing, mister?" Kelly said.

"If I was, I reckon I could get you before you laid a hand on that Colt of yours still stuck nice and firm in that gun belt yonder," the man answered.

"Colt? Gun belt? Oh, that. I just use that gun belt to keep my pants up. My ma always did say I was too skinny to hold up my own britches."

"Yeah? Then just what would you intend on doin' to stop me if I was of a mind to draw down on you?"

"Move any closer to that Remington of yours, and you'll find out." Kelly's eyes grew serious, and the friendly smile was gone.

The man began to fidget. He stretched his fingers as if he needed to make sure they were limber enough for what he was thinking of doing.

Kelly slowly drew the blanket off his legs with his left hand, revealing the Winchester pointing directly at the man.

Sweat broke out on the gunman's face as he lifted his hand away from the Remington. "No need for gunplay, pardner; I ain't got a mind to do anythin' hasty. I'll just sit a spell, if you don't mind, and maybe have a taste of that coffee."

"Help yourself," said Kelly.

"Obliged." The man sat by the fire, lifted the small pot, and filled one of the two cups Kelly had placed on the ground. He raised it to his lips and took a sip of the steamy brew.

"And while you're at it, how about losing that hogleg and laying it where I can keep an eye on it? I think I'd feel more comfortable."

The man hesitated for a moment as his glance once again fell to the rifle pointing in his direction, then began unbuckling his gun belt. He rolled it up and set it on the ground several inches away from where he sat. He reached over to where he'd left his coffee on the ground, picked it up, and again sipped from the cup.

"Why have you been on my trail?" Kelly said.

The man suddenly got very nervous. "I—uh—don't

kn-know what you're talkin' about, mister. I ain't been followin' you or no one else, neither. I was, uh, out lookin' for strays. That's all."

"Not much of that low desert is fit for cattle. They mostly just end up with a mouthful of cactus barbs."

The man looked away quickly. Kelly saw him searching for his next story.

"What's your handle?"

The man let out a sigh of resignation. "George Alvord."

"So, what are you really doing out here all alone, George?"

It was difficult for Kelly to think of the scraggly man sitting across the fire from him as a gunman. That didn't mean he wasn't dangerous, but he was too shaky, too sloppy in his mannerisms to have ever been successful at drawing down on another man face-to-face. But there was no question he was hiding something, and a man with a secret was a man not to be trusted.

"I guess you could say I'm sort of a drifter. Ain't headed anyplace in particular, and ain't really *from* anyplace, neither. How about yourself?"

"Reckon I'm just driftin' a little myself," said Kelly.

The conversation was going nowhere, and it was clear Alvord wasn't going to be forthcoming, which meant there was no way of knowing the man's intentions. This put Kelly into a tough situation. He couldn't very well roll over and go to sleep, for fear he might not wake up in the morning.

He studied the man's face. Then he said, "You aren't wanted someplace, are you?"

"Me? Why, no. I'm just a down-on-my-luck cowboy tryin' to scratch out a livin' pushin' beeves wherever I can find work. And that's the gospel truth."

"Tell you what, Mr. Alvord, I wouldn't mind at all if you'd just bed down here for the night. You can move on in the morning."

"Naw, couldn't impose. I'll just be gettin' on right after a couple more sips of your coffee."

Kelly raised the rifle again, aiming it directly at the man. "That wasn't a suggestion. Now kick that gun belt over here, and hold out your arms."

"W-what's goin' on here? I didn't do nothin' to you."

"You'll be spendin' the night shackled to that paloverde over there. I need a good night's rest, and I don't want to be wonderin' whether you're sneakin' back in here to plug me," said Kelly.

"I ain't no dry-gulcher."

"I have only your word on that, and I can't afford to take chances."

Alvord started to protest, then thought better of it when Kelly's vest fell open and he got his first view of the marshal's badge pinned to his shirt, gleaming in the firelight. The glum resignation that crept across Alvord's face suggested he and the law hadn't always been on the friendliest of terms.

An hour before dawn, just as the night prepared to relinquish its hold, Kelly was awakened by the sound of boots on loose gravel. As he blinked to adjust to the dim light, he saw a vague, shadowy figure about fifteen feet away, coming toward him. He threw off the blanket and grabbed the rifle. He got off one shot before the figure scrambled behind a boulder with a yelp. He went on the chase after whoever it was who had come calling, but he found no sign of him, only a few drops of blood trailing away. Returning, he tossed some dry grass and a few small pieces of wood onto the fire to get it built up quickly. He called out to Alvord, who appeared to have slept through the events of the past few minutes, gunshot and all. He trotted over to see how the man had fared after being shackled all night. He slid to a stop on the gravel.

"Alvord, wake up," he called, reaching down to shake his shoulder. "Hey!"

The man was still slumped over, leaning against the trunk of the tree. But he wasn't sleeping. The splash of blood across the front of his shirt was the first sign that Alvord hadn't spent a very restful night at all.

He was dead.

Kelly knelt beside Alvord's body. The man had been stabbed.

"How could this have happened with me not fifteen feet away?" Kelly mumbled, barely able to accept that he had been moments away from the same fate.

He looked around for Alvord's gun. It was still lying near Kelly's bedroll, so the killer hadn't come any farther into the camp than it took to kill Alvord and attempt the same on Kelly. But something *was* missing:

the victim's saddlebags, the ones he had held so closely to his side when he rode in. They had been right next to him when he went to sleep.

Kelly was angry at himself for letting this gruesome killing happen only feet away from where he had slept so soundly. He felt guilty for the man's death yet saw no other way he could have handled a situation that seemed untenable at best.

"I don't know who you were or where you came from, mister, but I'm going to find out," he said as he began digging a shallow grave for Alvord's body.

Before burying him, he went through the pockets of Alvord's worn pants and shirt. There were no identifying documents, no hint of his past, nothing to attest to his having lived a life at all. Afterward, Kelly located the man's horse. He looked over the saddle for any sign of where Alvord had come from, to no avail. One thing Kelly did notice was that Alvord's horse had one shoe nearly broken in half. The mangled remains, while somehow not affecting the horse's gait, left a clear and unmistakable trail. He suddenly realized why Alvord had been dogging him. *This man was on the run and knew his own trail was too easily followed. He needed another horse. He must have figured an exchange of mounts at gunpoint would be a smart move.*

But Kelly needed to know why Alvord was apparently running from something or somebody. Since there was only one way to get those answers, he mounted up and, leading Alvord's horse, began the arduous task of backtracking the trail of the mysterious man who'd met his death during the night at the hands of someone with more than a passing interest in Alvord and whatever was in his saddlebags.

Kelly kicked himself for not being more curious about those bags when Alvord rode in.

Chapter Two

The tiny town of Liberty had few things to recommend it to investors and was even less appealing to visitors. It got its start when a stamp mill was built to handle ore from the several upstart mines in the area, but many had since played out or saw barely enough pay dirt to keep them open. A few scattered mines were still in operation, but none produced sufficient quantities of color to attract any big speculators. And, although it still served as a stopover for cattle drovers pushing an occasional herd between the border and Tucson, the town got little business from surrounding small ranches that had found it too difficult to raise any substantial herds on the meager grasses of the area. Water was also scarce, leaving only a handful of ranches able to survive. Liberty seemed destined to remain a dusty desert crossing with two saloons, a modest bank, three stores, a livery, a restaurant, and a blacksmith. At least the weekly stagecoach from Fort Bowie to Tucson was still running, making its regular stops in Liberty, Cochise, and a couple of relay stations in between.

The law rested firmly in the hands of Sheriff Emmett Drago, a onetime gunman, and his handpicked deputy, Cloyd. Almost two years earlier, Drago had brought his new wife, Flower, to Liberty to settle down in what she hoped would be a blessed state of holy matrimony. At least that had been Flower's dream.

But neither matrimony, blessed or otherwise, nor the town's business climate were uppermost in the minds of the sheriff and his deputy that morning.

"I hope ol' Alvord is happy wherever he is," said Drago.

"It seemed a fool thing to do, lettin' them two just take off with half the money," answered Cloyd, a seedy little man Drago had saved from being hanged by a group of vigilantes down near the border. Cloyd had been suspected of being a rustler, and a fair amount of evidence was presented to support the allegation. Drago came along at just the right moment, freed the man at the point of a shotgun, and gained himself a friend for life, like it or not. "Him and his worthless friend demandin' their share and then leavin' wasn't right."

"Every man has an itch he needs to scratch. Alvord just picked a darn fool time to scratch his," said Drago. "And don't you never question my decisions again."

Cloyd scooted farther down in his chair and yawned. "Where'd you put ours?"

"I got it hid away nice and safe—don't you worry."

"You know I ain't worried—just curious, that's all."

"Too much curiosity can shorten a man's life," said Drago.

Cloyd nodded, then stood to leave.

"Where you goin'?" asked Drago.

"To have myself a shot of somethin' stronger than your coffee," said Cloyd, "Then I might hit the bunk for a spell."

Drago grunted his approval of the deputy taking his leave. He had never been all that fond of Cloyd, but he kept him around because, in a tough spot, the man had proven to be pretty good with a Colt .45, an attribute the sheriff needed to bring to mind often as he struggled to overlook the almost overwhelming odor that clung to the scruffy gunman like stink on a skunk. In fact, Drago had to admit that Cloyd bore a distinct similarity to that striped critter. He couldn't recall ever having seen the man get friendly with water and a bar of soap.

Drago decided he'd slip home for a while himself. He hadn't been home for over thirty-seven hours, and his wife would be wondering where he'd been. He hung a sign on the office door in case an emergency came up, locked up, and strolled the dusty street up the hill to his house.

On a little overlook at the edge of town, Drago had built—with the town's money, of course—a small clapboard-sided house with a double fireplace that served both of the two main rooms. On the back, he'd added a tiny kitchen at the request of his new bride, a dance hall girl he'd met in a Tombstone saloon. She became attracted to him when she witnessed him face down Curley Bill Brocius in a barroom confrontation. The fact that Curley Bill was so drunk that he couldn't have hit his own foot in no way diminished Flower's admiration for Drago's nerve. In fact, Drago was also drunk when he asked Flower to marry him, but she discounted that and clung to him, determined to take advantage of her first real chance to escape a life few "painted ladies" survived more than a handful of years.

But once she was settled down in Liberty, Flower discovered that Emmett Drago was less than eager to be tamed by a woman, and she found her life turning more miserable by the day. She struggled to avoid her husband's violent, liquor-sodden outbursts, to sidestep the physical punishment to which she had fallen victim so many times, but his failure to answer her questions about his late-night escapades often brought a sarcastic response from her, which could in itself trigger his wrath.

When he eased open the door, he was met by the smell of bacon cooking in a skillet and the sight of Flower standing in the kitchen, vigorously whipping something in a big clay bowl, humming to herself.

She looked up and smiled as he entered. "Didn't hear you leave this mornin', hon. I must have been sound asleep."

Drago wasn't fooled. He knew she could be awakened instantly by the mere sound of a cockroach skittering across the floor, but he dismissed her attempt to get him to fess up and went along for the ride.

"Yeah. Couldn't sleep, so I went out early to check on the town," he said.

"Probably a good thing too. It's a dangerous community. Let's see, we had a dog go rabid about a year back, and then there was that window got busted at Cleary's store by a rock kicked up by a wagon," she mused with a sly grin.

"I know you don't think there's much happenin' around here, but that's because no one wants to test my hand with this .45." He patted the well-used Colt revolver residing in the holster that hung at his side.

Flower said nothing, just kept on humming and began kneading dough for biscuits. She had pressed as hard as she dared—unless, of course, she pined for another black eye. She'd been beaten enough times to know just how far to push her husband. From his snapped response, she knew she had already reached that limit. Her ability to read men was the result of several years of working in a saloon, having to match wits with some of the worst hard cases in the Arizona Territory.

"I'll have some biscuits ready in a few minutes. Coffee's hot if you'd like some now," she said, giving up her attempt to find out why her husband was spending so much time away from home lately.

Drago just grunted, took off his gun belt, and slumped into a chair. His mind was neither on coffee nor on Flower's ever-present curiosity. He was deep in thought about recent actions that *could* cost him everything . . . even his life.

Piedmont Kelly reined in his horse at a small, barely trickling stream and dismounted. He let both horses drink as he wiped his brow with a handkerchief. The morning sun was beating down with its usual intensity, baking everything in sight. *Desert animals are smart enough to seek shade. Only a human is dumb enough to wander around without a known destination and no plan for when he gets there.* He shook his head as he patted his horse's withers.

Alvord's horse's tracks were surprisingly clear and easy to follow. It was no wonder whoever had been tracking him had no trouble finding him. Even in moonlight it would have been easy. Last night had fit the bill perfectly for such an evil deed, with clear skies and a full moon.

The sound of rocks skittering down an incline caught Kelly's attention fast. He spun around and drew his recently purchased single-action Army Colt. Seeing nothing, he carefully picked his way along the stream to where the sound seemed to have come from. He saw nothing and, assuming it had been a rabbit or a coyote, holstered his weapon and started back to where his horse was still slurping up what little water he could find. Then another sound drifted through the still air. It sounded like the groan of a wounded animal. He investigated farther up the side of the hill. What he found was no wounded animal but an old man, an Indian, lying facedown in the dirt. He appeared to be a Chiricahua Apache, the tribe of Cochise and Geronimo.

Kelly moved slowly toward the man, who was sprawled out as if he'd fallen while attempting to reach water. But it wasn't just thirst that had brought the man down; the bloom of blood on his shirt suggested he was badly injured. The Indian made an attempt to roll away as Kelly approached, but he was too weak from loss of blood to move more than a few inches. A knife was stuck in the cloth belt wrapped around his thin waist. With a gnarled and bloody hand he grasped the hilt but was unable to draw the blade even to protect himself.

"Take it easy, old man. I'm just tryin' to help you."

The Indian grunted. Fear in his eyes showed his lack of trust in this white man, but there was little he could do to ward off any danger. His strength was sapped. He appeared to have been in the wilderness for a time, for his legs and arms were caked with dried blood, likely from stumbling and falling often. The pain in his eyes spoke of an ordeal he had probably survived only by dogged determination. And even that was about to leave him. Kelly could see that the old man had been felled by a bullet that had struck him in the lower back.

Kelly bent down, rolled the man over, pulled the knife from the Indian's belt, and tossed it aside. He was wise enough not to try to attend to the man's wounds without taking care not to present an obvious opportunity to a potential enemy.

Peeling back the bloody shirt, he saw that he'd have

his hands full if there was any chance of saving the old man's life. He lifted the frail body and carried him down to the creek to make him as comfortable as possible, then began picking up dead branches from around the small shrubs and trees that lined the only source of water for miles. He built a fire to get his knife searing hot to seal the wound after he dug the bullet out.

It would be touch-and-go for the old Indian, and Kelly knew he had little time to waste. He set about the task without knowing whether he'd end up burying the Indian after all his efforts. But he had to try. He placed a stick in the Indian's mouth and told him to bite down.

"This is gonna hurt bad, old man. But it's the only chance you've got. I have to get the bullet out. Do you understand?"

The Indian nodded weakly, then passed out as Kelly dug out the bullet and tossed it into the dirt. Blood was gushing from the wound, and Kelly knew he had to cauterize it. He thrust his knife blade deeper into the coals, and when it was almost glowing itself, he placed the blade across the wound, closing it as if he had just branded a steer. The smell of burning flesh struck his nostrils with a nauseating sting. If he was a betting man, he'd bet against the odds of the weak old man's making it through the night.

Before bedding down, Kelly checked the bandage he'd used to cover the angry wound. He'd torn a strip off the bottom of an old shirt he'd been too stingy to throw away. Soaking it in some whiskey from a flask in his saddlebags, he'd placed it where it would protect the wound from dirt or curious insects. He'd then washed the blood off the man's arms and legs as best he could.

The entire ordeal took him back nearly two years, when he, too, had been shot in the back and left for dead, lying facedown in the dirt. If it hadn't been for a strong woman driving a work wagon coming along at just the right moment, willing to help, he knew he'd have died. The thought of dying alone in no-man's-land sent a shiver up his back, and he felt somehow he had been chosen to help this similarly stricken man.

As the day waned, Kelly settled down near the fire to await whatever the new day brought. He drifted off into a troubled sleep, feeling that death itself hovered over the old Indian.

Chapter Three

Drago didn't go straight back to the shanty he called an office that afternoon after storming out of the house. He was tired of sparring with Flower over where he'd spent nearly two days and nights. She knew he hadn't been out checking the town for the misdeeds of local villains, but he wasn't the least bit interested in either her opinion or her attempts to keep his comings and goings under her control. So he saddled his horse and rode down the middle of the town's only street and straight out into the hilly wilderness. He kept looking back to make certain he wasn't being followed, something he wouldn't put past Cloyd. After determining he was alone on the trail, he prodded his mount down into a steep ravine, across a small clearing, and disappeared into the crumbling entrance of a long-abandoned mine about two miles south of town.

Inside, Drago tied his horse to a large, rusty spike jutting from one of the timbers that kept the sides of the tunnel from collapsing. He looked about once more for any sign of unwanted visitors; then, satisfied he was alone, he touched a match to the wick of a lantern and began to make his way back into the dark shaft.

After several minutes of following the mine's underground passage deep into the side of a rocky hill, Drago came to a point where the tunnel split off in two directions. The floor of the route he took stood about an inch deep in bluish green water that was slowly leaching from the walls. The air was damp and close and smelled of rotting wood and sulfur. He finally came to a place where some timbers had collapsed, letting tons of rock and dirt nearly cut off the tunnel ahead. A small opening could be seen through the debris, where someone had cleared away some stones and dirt, providing a passage just large enough for a medium-size man to get through.

Struggling through the tightness of the tiny clearing and gasping from the nearly suffocating absence of any sort of ventilation, Drago sucked great gulps of stale air into his lungs just to keep from passing out from lack of oxygen. As he cleared the hole, he slumped against the damp wall for a moment to catch his breath. He held the lantern up to locate a crevice in the wall, far back in the shadows. He scooted over to the narrow opening and reached in, pulled out a pair of saddlebags, and dropped them to the ground.

Squatting next to the bags, he lifted the flap of one and

spilled out a portion of the contents. *This is going to make me the king of this whole valley,* he thought, nearly bursting with excitement. *People will tip their hats when I walk by, and women will swoon at the thought of my bringing them flowers. I'll own everything in sight and live in style.* Then his thoughts turned to his wife, and his expression grew as dark as the cave in which he sat hunkered down on his haunches.

"I reckon I'll just have to tell all those admirin' females that my poor wife is recently deceased!" he shouted to the walls. "And maybe I'll just have to make that come true if she can't learn to keep her mouth shut!"

His words echoed down the long passageway as he let out a demonic laugh.

As dawn broke over the desert, Kelly sat by the fire, now little more than a heap of hot coals. The Indian had spent a fitful night, and the marshal hadn't held out much hope that the withered old man would survive until morning. But survive he did, and he was now showing signs of coming to. The old man was uttering occasional moans that became stronger as he thrashed around under the blanket Kelly had wrapped around him. The man's eyelids fluttered, then opened. A mixture of fear, pain, and puzzlement came over him as he tried to lift himself up on one arm.

"Hold on, friend. You've got a ways to go before you can get up and walk out of here. Just take a drink of this water. You'll feel better," said Kelly.

The Indian sipped from the canteen held to his lips.

His fear seemed to abate somewhat as he eased back, puffing from the exertion.

"You need rest to get your strength back," Kelly said.

"Who are you, *Bedalpago*?" the Indian mumbled.

A grin came across Kelly's face. He knew *Bedalpago* was the Apache word for an Anglo with a mustache. It meant *hairy mouth.* He unconsciously tugged at his own lip adornment.

"My name is Piedmont Kelly. I'm a marshal. I came upon you yesterday. You had a serious gunshot wound. I dug out the bullet and patched you up as best I could. Who shot you?"

The man searched the sky as if for a memory, anything that would bring back the reason for his present state of affairs. Apparently unable to gather his thoughts, he closed his eyes and lay still.

"That's okay. You just stay there and get some rest. I'll try to find some food," said Kelly. He got up, took his rifle, and left camp.

When he returned half an hour later with two rabbits tied together with a rawhide string and slung over his shoulder, he found the old man half sitting up. He was holding the canteen.

"I take more of your water," the Indian said with a raspy voice.

"You're welcome to all the water you want. I was able to bag us something to eat."

"I am grateful. I will repay you."

"You owe me nothing. A fella shouldn't seek a reward for helpin' a man in need."

Kelly built up the fire before he began skinning the rabbits, and soon he had them skewered on a stick and hung over the fire. The smell of meat cooking seemed to bring strength to the Indian, who looked as if he hadn't eaten for days.

"It was my own people," the Indian said.

Kelly looked at him quizzically, as if the man was talking in riddles.

"My people shot me as a traitor."

"Oh. Why did they think you had betrayed them?" Kelly said.

"I was a policeman on the reservation for the Apache. When the white-eyes colonel thought I had become too old, he sent me back to live with my people. My chief said I had betrayed the trust of all Apaches by serving the white man's soldiers. He sent me out with some others from the reservation to hunt for food, and one of them shot me. Left me to die."

Kelly pulled apart one of the steaming rabbits and handed it to the Indian. The man nodded as he took it, tearing into it as one who was famished. Kelly wasn't quite sure what to do with the man. He couldn't just let him wander the desert; sooner or later an Army patrol would spot him and send him back to the reservation. He didn't want to have saved the man's life only to see it forfeited by placing him back in the same situation he'd already been lucky to survive. He also didn't want to be playing nursemaid to an old Indian who would surely slow him down as he tried to track Alvord's horse. *The situation will just have to play itself out,* thought Kelly.

"What are you called, old man?"

"Spotted Dog."

"You've come a long way from the San Carlos. How did you make it this far with a bullet in your back?"

"I was climbing a ridge along the Tortillas when the shot came from behind. I do not remember what happened after that."

Kelly was confused by what the old man said. They were still a ways west of the Tortilla range, and a man as badly wounded as Spotted Dog could have made it this far only with great strength and deliberation. Kelly's suspicion that the truth was being treated with little regard only added to his consternation as to what to do with his new companion. The desert was dotted with small towns, and he figured his best bet would be to continue tracking Alvord's horse as long as possible, counting on the possibility that one of the villages along the way might have a doctor.

"Spotted Dog, I have an extra horse. Tomorrow you can ride it until we come to a place where you will be safe and a doctor can look at your wound," said Kelly.

Spotted Dog didn't stop eating long enough to acknowledge Kelly's offer with anything more than a grunt.

It was midafternoon when Drago returned to town, tying his horse in front of the sheriff's office. Cloyd was out front in a chair leaning back against the wall.

"Where you been, Sheriff? The missus said you left early this morning."

"Where I go and what I do is none of your business, Cloyd. Flower's, neither. You understand?"

"Sure. Didn't mean to get you riled. Just makin' conversation."

"Well, make some kind of conversation other than meddlin' in my affairs," Drago said as he stomped up the steps to the weather-worn building and went inside, slapping at his clothing to rid himself of trail dust. The glass in the door rattled its disapproval of being slammed shut.

Cloyd noticed mud on Drago's pants and a bluish stain on his boots. He was smart enough not to make a comment, but he was about to explode with curiosity. *What's that man been sloshin' around in to get his boots all blue?* he thought.

Cloyd decided he'd go have himself a beer and think this all out, so he told Drago he'd be back later and left to cross the street to the Silver Strike Saloon.

"Hey, Cloyd, come on over and pull up a chair. Have a beer," said the only other patron in the saloon, a stubby man with a great gray beard and a belly that hung down over his belt like a bag of oats.

"No, thanks, Devlin. Need to be by myself a spell and do some thinkin'."

"Suit yourself, Deputy, but I was thinkin' I might even buy."

"Oh, all right." Cloyd scooted a chair up to the table that Devlin was leaning on with both elbows. Three empty glasses sat in front of him. He raised a hand and called to the bartender to bring two more beers.

"What you got that's so all-fired important to think about anyway, Cloyd? There ain't nothin' in this godforsaken place worth spit nor consideration, an' you know it," Devlin said as the beers were set in from of them.

"Sometimes a body just has to be alone to sort things out."

"Now, what you got to sort out? You cain't have no women problems, 'cause there ain't no unmarried women here 'cept them two gals singin' at the saloon and the widder Brenden. And the widder is old enough to be your ma."

"I got to conjure up where a fella could hide something so secret that the findin' of it could make a man rich beyond belief," said Cloyd. The very second he said it, he knew he'd said more than he should have. If Drago found out he'd let a hint of their secret slip from his lips, it could get him killed.

Devlin's next words confirmed the foolishness of the deputy's loose tongue. "I cain't say I know of such a place, but I'll ask Sheriff Drago the very next time I see him. He's the smartest man in town."

Chapter Four

Retracing the tracks of Alvord's horse was proving to be fairly easy. For that, Kelly was thankful. For the most part, the hoofprints remained distinct, easily standing apart from any other tracks. The trail did, however, take some strange turns and twists, occasionally switching from well-used, wagon-rutted roads to stretches of hilly, cactus-laden scrub strewn with slickrock and gopher holes. It was obvious Alvord had purposely varied the course he took, as if he feared he, too, was being followed. If so, it was obvious that Alvord had a right to be nervous. While finding parts of the terrain the dead man had traversed more difficult than others, Kelly also knew he must take care to make the trip as easy as possible so as not to worsen the old Apache's condition.

Spotted Dog seemed strong of will for a man of his

age and physical plight. It was a wonder to Kelly that this spindly old soul could have survived such a heinous wound and less than two days later appear to be continuing on almost as if he had never been shot. Almost. But Kelly knew that looks could be deceiving.

"Do you need to stop and rest, old man?"

"No need. I grow stronger."

"We'll stop soon and let you rest, anyway. This is rough country for a man who just had a bullet dug out of him. I admire your strength, though," said Kelly.

"Village at foot of mountain of my ancestors, there," he said, pointing. "You leave me there."

"Do they have a doctor?"

"Have no need of medicine man now. You have given me back life when I was already dead. You have kept my spirit from leaving me."

"Just the same, I want to have a doctor look at you."

Spotted Dog tried his best to look the part of a healthy man, but Kelly saw the pain in his eyes and his inability to sit straight in the saddle. He lolled from side to side with the gait of the horse as if he were little more than tall grass blowing in the wind.

Cloyd was anxious about what he had said to Devlin at the saloon. He knew Drago would be spitting mad if he found out his own deputy couldn't keep his mouth shut, especially concerning something as important as where his and Drago's ill-gotten bounty might be hidden.

Why did Drago feel the need to be in charge of the loot, anyway? Even more important, why had he hidden it without letting his deputy know where? It was almost as if the sheriff didn't trust him or, worse, was planning on cutting him out of the prize altogether. Either way, it wasn't sitting well with Cloyd. He was rolling these thoughts around in his mind when he nearly ran smack into Flower as she stepped out of the dry goods store. The sunlight danced off strands of blond hair that peeked out from beneath her bonnet. While Flower's youth was now well behind her, she was still a striking woman, one men never failed to notice whenever she walked the dusty street of Liberty.

"Why, 'scuse me, Miz Flower. Sorry I nearly run you down. I'm afraid my head was off wanderin' somewheres else." Cloyd tipped his hat and gave her a yellow-toothed smile.

Flower struggled to return a grimacing smile. She detested the scruffy deputy and had on more than one occasion tried to convince her husband that it would make him look better if he hired someone more suitable as his assistant. Emmett had insisted each time that whom he hired was his business and none of hers. She brushed by Cloyd without a word, her disgust with his filthy appearance barely hidden behind a facade of propriety.

Cloyd went on his way, muttering to himself about uppity people who thought they were too good for others. He was also thinking about how he could take back his ill-timed question to Devlin and what he'd do if Drago found out. *What if Devlin really does go to the sheriff with my stupid question?* He shook his head in disgust at his situation but came up with no practical answer.

On his way to the sheriff's office, Cloyd saw Devlin heading to the same destination. Determined to steer him clear of Drago, Cloyd called out. "Hey, Devlin. What say we have a beer? I'm buyin' this time."

Devlin stopped dead in his tracks at the prospect of a free drink. "Wouldn't miss an opportunity like that, Cloyd."

They walked together into the Silver Strike Saloon, found a table, and got comfortable, as if neither of them had a thing in the world more important to do than spend time sopping up warm beer in the middle of the day. After the bartender left two foamy glasses on the table, Cloyd insisted the two toast to better times and a new silver strike.

"You know that silly question I asked you about a place to hide something of value?" Cloyd said.

"Yeah, sure. And I said I'd ask Sheriff Drago the next time I saw him. I was headin' over to ask him that very question," said Devlin.

"Well, see, you can't do that, because it would take away the surprise. I was plannin' to give him and Flower a present for bein' so nice to me, and since I sleep in that stinkin' little storage room over the general store, I don't got no place to hide a gift. You do see that, don't you?"

"Oh, I get it. You want me to keep a secret. Sure, Cloyd, sure. I can do that for a friend. My mouth is shut tight—don't you never fear."

Inside, Cloyd was jumping up and down that he had been able to turn his mistake into a way to save his skin. Devlin wasn't very bright, but he always had been amiable enough, and Cloyd figured he could be trusted. Besides, other than killing him and dumping his body in the ravine outside of town, what choice did he have but to give simple lying a try? Cloyd let out a sigh and then leaned back to gulp down his glass of beer.

"You know, I *have* been thinkin' on what you said, and the only decent hidin' place I could conjure up in this old head is that abandoned mine down at the bottom of the ravine. Plenty of secret places there you could hide your present," said Devlin.

Cloyd sat up straight. *Yes,* he thought, *that's it. That makes sense. That bluish stain on Drago's boots, the mud on his pants . . . the old mine. That's got to be where he hid it.*

"Devlin, you're a genius. That's perfect. Here, let me treat you to another beer." He tossed a dime onto the table. "But remember, not a word to no one." Cloyd kicked back his chair and headed out of the saloon with a broad smile on his face.

The little town of Cochise was mostly wooden buildings, a few adobes, and more than fifteen canvas-covered frame structures. The town didn't appear so new as it did temporary. Each day a mine closed, and each day another one opened. No one could count on being there for more than a couple of years, more or less. Kelly asked a wagon driver the whereabouts of the doctor's office and was told the physician was about as likely to be at the saloon as at his office.

"And where can I find the sheriff?"

"More than likely *he's* taking his afternoon nap. Office is just down the street 'bout a half block, on the right."

Kelly thanked the man and, with Spotted Dog on Alvord's horse following closely, rode slowly down the wide street. A freight wagon rattled past them, kicking up dust as it went. Kelly and Spotted Dog reined up in front of the sheriff's office, and the marshal helped the old Indian off Alvord's horse and up the steps to the boardwalk.

Upon opening the door, Kelly was surprised to see an old friend, John Henry Stevens, a longtime lawman in the Territory. The sheriff awoke at the sound of boots on the creaky wooden floor.

"What can I do for you?" said Stevens, rubbing his eyes after being so rudely awakened.

"You can say howdy to an old friend, John Henry," said Kelly, thrusting his hand forward.

"Well, I'll be a ring-tailed bobcat, if it ain't Piedmont Kelly. Why, I thought you'd have had enough of workin' for the government and settled into a soft sheriffin' job in some little out-of-the-way burg where the closest thing to a gunshot is some hurrahin' on the Fourth of July." Stevens took Kelly's hand and shook it enthusiastically.

"Like here in Cochise?"

Stevens laughed. "Yeah, just like. What brings you here, anyway? I thought marshals stuck pretty close to the excitement. Ain't none of that here. What are you doing in Cochise?"

"I need a doctor to look at this man's wound. He was shot. I patched him up as best I could, but . . . say, those cells got decent beds in them?"

"Yep."

"Okay, I'd like for the Indian to lay down and get some rest. I'll want your doctor to look at him as soon as possible too."

"Say, who is that Injun?"

"Name's Spotted Dog."

Stevens moved to grab a ring of keys off a wooden peg behind his desk and hand them to his deputy, who had just come in the door. "Jed, put this Indian in the first cell, where we can keep an eye on him. Didn't you say you'd recognize him?"

"Yes, sir, Sheriff, that's him, all right. I've seen him before," said Jed.

Kelly was puzzled.

The deputy took Spotted Dog by one arm and led him back into a room where three cells occupied the rear of the brick building.

"Well, this calls for a celebration, Kelly. We'll toast your bringin' in one badly wanted killer and robber. Drinks are on me. Fine job, old friend," said Stevens after the Indian was settled in the back.

"Hold on, John Henry. What's all this about this man bein' a killer and a robber?"

"You mean you don't know? Well, I'll tell you everything over a beer," said Stevens. "And I'll have someone fetch the doctor. Best that Injun be in good health when we hang him."

"John Henry, there'll be no talk about hangin' until you tell me what's happened to make you think this man is a killer."

"Fair enough, Marshal."

Kelly went back to see that Spotted Dog had settled onto a rickety wooden bed. Kelly told the old man to lie back and there'd be a doctor to see him. The Indian just nodded, barely able to keep his head up after the exhausting ride in blistering heat. Stevens insisted the deputy lock the door to the cell, even though Kelly scowled at the idea.

When they got to the saloon, Stevens pointed them to a corner table where they could talk without being overheard. He called for the bartender to bring over some beer in a pitcher and a couple of glasses.

He leaned forward on the table after the bartender left. "Late last week, Sheriff Drago over in Liberty found the Overland Stage off the road just west of his town. The driver and his guard were gunned down, two passengers shot dead, and the money box had been taken. The bank in Tucson says there was ten thousand dollars on that stage intended for Fort Bowie," said Stevens.

"What's that got to do with the Indian?"

"I'm comin' to that. Drago said he and a posse tracked the robbers—a buncha Injuns—to a place along the San Pedro where they had camped. It was late in the day, and I suppose the thieves didn't expect to be tracked so soon. They put up a fight, but Drago and his men killed four of them; a fifth one got away but was wounded. He's the one they figured took the cash with him. They ain't found hide nor hair of him yet—that is, until you just walked him right into town, pretty as you please." Stevens lifted his beer as if to toast the marshal.

"You're sayin' Spotted Dog was one of the robbers?"

"The sheriff's description to my deputy of the Injun what got away fits with the man you brought in. Unfortunately, I was out of town at the time when it all happened."

"How did this Drago know his name?"

"Drago brought in a rifle with the name Spotted Dog carved right there on the stock. Said he found it where the Injun dropped it as he made his escape. Them Injuns take a lot of pride in their rifles; they want everybody to know what's theirs. Sorta like a callin' card."

Chapter Five

"Drago, I ain't aimin' to get you all riled up, but I think we ought to find a good, secure place to hide the money until things cool down," said Cloyd. The sheriff was leaning back in his chair, looking over a wanted dodger with Cloyd's picture on it. One hundred dollars was the reward, and they wanted him for cattle rustling down near Bisbee. Drago grinned as he folded the paper without showing it to Cloyd. *This could come in handy someday,* he thought.

"Don't you worry none about that money. It's safe where it is, and none of it leaves its hidin' place until I say so."

"But . . ."

"But nothin', Cloyd. The way I see it, you got two choices here: Either you trust me, or you don't. If you do, you'll keep your mouth shut, go on about your business, and wait until it's safe to let it see the light of day again. If you don't, you're welcome to try out that .45 on me. It's all up to you."

"Aw, Drago, I don't mean nothin' like that. It's just, well, you know, hard not knowin' it's safely hidden away and all, especially after the chance we took."

"I told you before, Cloyd, but I'll tell you again: We got this one down tighter than a rusty jar lid. Ain't nobody gonna find out what we did or where the money is stashed, and when it's safe, you and me'll be splittin' a tidy sum."

"Just how much, you figure?"

Drago thought about that for a minute before answering. He knew Cloyd couldn't read the newspaper, but he might have heard something about the amount stolen from the stagecoach. If there was a way to hedge a little, give Cloyd a much smaller share, well, that would be just fine. But he had to be careful about what he said, in case Cloyd knew more than he let on and was just testing the sheriff.

"I ain't had time to count it yet. Somewheres around four thousand dollars, I reckon. Won't know exactly until I can count it out into piles. Don't make any difference right now, because we daren't start spreadin' it around yet. And another thing: If you open your mouth, just once, I'll shut it permanently. You understand?"

"You needn't worry none about me, Drago. Better to worry about Alvord and that cousin of his keepin' quiet."

Cloyd turned and walked out of the sheriff's office and down the street to his sleeping quarters, a small, windowless room above the general store.

Cloyd knew the sheriff would try holding out on him, but he didn't know what to do about it. He couldn't dry-gulch him without first knowing for certain where the money was. But now he had a suspicion, and he was planning to go there in the middle of the night to see if he was right.

Marshal Piedmont Kelly was deep in thought as he and Sheriff Stevens ambled back to the jail. Stevens had asked the lady at the dressmaker's shop next door to his office to fetch the doctor for the Indian. As the two approached the sheriff's door, they were nearly run over by the corpulent doctor hurrying out the door, the smell of whiskey on his breath.

"Ah, Sheriff, there you are. I've looked your man over, and he seems to be healing well from his wound. Whoever extracted that bullet did a fine piece of work. If you run into him, tell him I could always use an assistant."

"Tell him yourself, Doc. This here's U.S. Marshal Piedmont Kelly. He's the fella that patched up the Indian and brung him in."

Kelly and the doctor shook hands.

"Doctor, is there anything else the patient will be needin', and can he travel?"

"Whoa, Marshal," stammered Stevens. "Folks around here are gonna expect a trial and probably a hangin'. You can't just up and haul his carcass out of town."

"Sorry, John Henry, but there's more to this than meets the eye. I can't leave him here, and I have to find out more about the horse Spotted Dog rode in on. It belonged to a dead man by the name of George Alvord, and the Indian had nothin' to do with that. In fact, I'm pretty certain Alvord was runnin' away from somethin' himself."

"You ain't suggestin' this Alvord fella had anything to do with the stagecoach robbery, are you? Five Indians did it; that's what Sheriff Drago over in Liberty said."

"This Alvord rode up on me near the end of the day when I was about to make camp. He was jittery, and he was totin' a pair of saddlebags that was stuffed full of somethin' he wouldn't let out of his sight. That generally means money."

"So you're sayin' maybe he could have run into the Indian and took it from him?" Stevens said.

"I don't know what to think. All I know is, the next morning I found Alvord dead. He had been stabbed and his saddlebags taken."

"Maybe the Indian killed him and took back the money," said Stevens.

"Then what happened to those saddlebags? The Indian didn't have them when I found him."

"Hmm. Puts a fella in a quandary, don't it?"

"I do know I need that Indian nearby. Don't worry. If I find that Spotted Dog was one of the robbers and killers, I'll bring him right back here for a trial. Now, Doc, about the old man."

"Get some food into him, and let him rest for a day or two, and I think he could travel. But if you jostle him around too much, the wound could open up, and he'll sure as shootin' bleed to death." The doctor nodded and began to saunter down the street, whistling some unrecognizable tune as he disappeared into the saloon. Spotted Dog was asleep when the two lawmen entered the jail.

"Two days could let the trail of that mare get cold, maybe too cold. Any chance you recognize that horse, John Henry?"

"Hmm. I didn't really get a good look at her." He got up and went outside to the bay mare that was tied to the rail next to Kelly's black gelding and began running his hands over the horse's flanks. He patted the horse on its shoulder, then returned inside.

"I can't be sure, but I have to admit that horse does look kinda familiar. Take her down to the livery, and see if Sam remembers her. He knows every horse that ever entered his corral."

Good idea, thought Kelly. *A good liveryman spots things most others don't when it comes to horseflesh. They know all the spooky traits a horse can have too, like favoring a nip at any unwary hand coming too close to its mouth, or backing up when someone is in a stall with it, trying to pin the man to a wall.* Kelly got up and sauntered out of the jail, leaving the sheriff to watch over the sleeping Indian.

As he approached the livery, he noticed two men across the street, standing back in the shadows, leaning on a cottonwood tree. They were Indians. Most likely either Papago or reservation Apache—he couldn't tell from the distance. They seemed interested in him, however; their eyes followed him as if he were an enemy walking into an ambush. He acted as if he hadn't noticed them and slowly ambled in to find the owner of the livery.

"Hello. Anyone here?"

"Be right with you. I'm in the loft," came a gravelly voice from somewhere deep in the bowels of the dark, two-story building. Tiny pieces of straw and dust filtered down from between the second-floor planking as a large man stomped his way down a narrow stairway and into the open room at the front of the building. "Howdy. Name's Sam Arrowsmith. What can I do for you?"

"Piedmont Kelly. I wondered if you'd take a look at a horse I have tied outside. I'm interested in knowin' if you recognize it."

"Glad to," said Arrowsmith, tossing aside a hay rake. He wasted no time as he lumbered out through the large double doors at the entrance. He walked around the bay a couple of times, checked it over carefully, then walked back to where Kelly leaned against the doorframe.

"Yep, I know that horse. It's owned by a fella over in Liberty by the name of Alvord. Just what are you doin' with his horse?"

Kelly pulled open his vest to reveal his marshal's badge.

"Oh. Somethin' happen to Alvord?"

"He's dead, and I want to take his horse back to any family he might have," said Kelly.

Arrowsmith rubbed his chin for a moment as he tried to recollect what he might know about Alvord. "You know, I can't rightly say I know much about him except that he was a friend of the sheriff over there in Liberty. I ain't sure, but I heard he had kin right here in Cochise, but I don't know who. Sorry to hear he's dead, though. Friendly fella, even if he *was* a might quick to finger that revolver on his hip."

"Did he spend much time around here?"

"He did come by a few times, left his horse with me, then spent the night playin' cards down the street," said Arrowsmith. "Almost always left broke, as I recall."

Kelly pondered what Arrowsmith had said about Alvord's being a friend of the sheriff in Liberty. He remembered that it was that very sheriff who had found the robbed stagecoach. Maybe he *could* wait a couple more days until Spotted Dog was up to traveling. No sense following that horse's tracks anymore, as he was now thinking that they would lead him straight to Liberty.

Just after midnight, Cloyd pulled on his jeans and boots and quietly made his way down the stairs at the back of the general store to where he'd left his horse tied to a tree. He needed to make sure no one saw him leave, so he untied the reins and walked his horse behind the buildings all the way to the edge of town. He was nervous that Drago might be keeping an eye on him. Cloyd knew he'd made too much of the fact that he didn't know where the money was hidden. He looked around constantly, hoping to catch any hint of his being watched, but he saw no indication that Drago was anywhere near. In fact, he could see an oil lamp still burning at the sheriff's office, and Drago's horse was tied out front. That was comforting.

He mounted up and rode quickly out of town toward the ravine where the old mine was located, looking back every couple of minutes to see if he was being followed. While he saw no one, he could feel the hair on the back of his neck standing up as a chill skittered up his spine.

Nearing the mine, he dismounted and hid his horse back in a stand of mesquite trees in a gathering of giant granite boulders about fifty yards from the entrance. He sat on his haunches for several minutes to make sure he was alone, constantly waving a hand in front of his face to drive away biting gnats. He heard only the sounds of night critters scurrying around in the dark, seeking out a meal. Just as he was about to duck into the mine, he thought he heard a strange sound coming from deep in the shaft. It sounded very much like a pick striking rock.

Cloyd fumbled in his pocket for the candle stub he'd brought along, struck a match, and touched it to the wick. The eerie, dancing light emanating from the flickering candle gave him little comfort as he began following the shaft deeper underground. The echoing ring of a pick became louder and louder.

Chapter Six

When Kelly returned to Sheriff Stevens' office, he revealed that he'd decided to stay in town until Spotted Dog could travel. Stevens had mixed emotions about the Indian's leaving at all and expressed his doubts as forcefully as he could. But he knew the marshal could take the Apache anytime he wished, since he was the one who had brought him in, and Spotted Dog was, by all rights, still in the marshal's custody. But Stevens also knew that the citizens of Cochise were concerned about the stagecoach robbery and killings and wanted to see someone pay for the crime. If he could get a conviction for such a heinous deed, he would be a shoo-in to win the upcoming election barely three months away.

Kelly wandered over to the small hotel to get a room for a couple of days. He was given one with a single cracked window that looked out on the street, a location subject to all the noise from rumbling wagons passing by and boisterous cowboys spending their meager dollars at the saloon, drinking and gambling. But rooms were at a premium, and he had to settle for what he could get. He plunked down his two bits and hauled his saddlebags into room number 6, a shabby cubbyhole with a narrow iron bed jammed against a wall, covered with a thin mattress laid atop a wire-strung frame. The flimsy pillow would afford little comfort, but it would be better than the hard ground. He stared briefly into a small Chatham mirror whose silver backing was beginning to separate from the glass, giving it a ghostly effect around the edges. He poured water into the china washbowl and bathed the desert grime off his face and hands. It was getting late in the day, and, feeling a twinge of hunger from the smell of food cooking throughout the town, he went across the street to a little restaurant, hoping for better fare than the sticks of beef jerky and bitter coffee he'd been living off for several days.

The sign in the window read MISS NETTIE'S HOME COOKING, and the tables all had tablecloths and little porcelain vases with a single flower sticking out of each. The wallpapered room was cheery despite the dust that swirled around everyone who opened the door to enter. A very pretty woman with long brown hair rolled up in a bun came over to his table and welcomed him. A single curly strand had escaped its confines and dangled lazily down her forehead.

Her smile sent a shiver of excitement through him. He was suddenly glad he'd bothered to wash up.

"Welcome, stranger. I'm Nettie. What can I get you? Specials are all written there," she said, pointing to a blackboard that hung on the wall near what he figured must be the door to the kitchen. Her voice was gentle, with a warm, midwestern accent—perhaps from Kansas or Missouri, he thought.

"I'll have the stew, a couple of biscuits, and some Arbuckle's," he said.

"I'll have it ready in a minute. Hope you're hungry. I made lots of stew, and I don't aim for it to go to waste," she said with a wink. Miss Nettie turned and—to Kelly, at least—seemed to float back into the kitchen.

Kelly stared after her for a moment, letting his imagination take him back to a time when he had the leisure to court a lady. That hadn't been for a long while. Her perfume seemed to linger at his table like a welcome guest.

Cloyd was as nervous as a steer in a thunderstorm as he slowly made his way back through the twists and turns of the mine tunnel. The sounds grew louder as he got closer to whatever or whoever it was picking away at the hard rock sides of the shaft. At first his thoughts conjured up Drago digging up their stash. Or maybe someone had gotten wind of its whereabouts and was looking for it. Either way, Cloyd was taking no chances. He had his .45 in his hand and fully cocked. The flickering candle gave him only enough light to see about ten feet in front of him, and the tunnel turned and twisted so often and so abruptly, he knew he could stumble onto whoever was in there with little or no prior notice. Sweat poured off his brow, running into his eyes and stinging, causing him to wipe at them constantly with a shirtsleeve.

Just as he crept around a bend, he saw the light from a lantern coming from a small, recently dug out place in the rock. A man was bent over, picking up chips of stone and examining each before tossing them into a pile. Startled by Cloyd's arrival, the man glanced about quickly, looking for some way to put up a defense, but his shotgun was leaning against the far wall, much too great a distance to cover before the deputy could drop him.

"Devlin! What are you doin' in here?" Cloyd said, shaken by finding his friend in the mine.

Devlin dropped his pick and held up his hands. "D-don't shoot, Cloyd. I ain't done nothin' wrong. Just lookin' for gold."

"Gold! You idiot. This mine is tapped out. Ain't no gold in here. And put your hands down. I ain't gonna plug you."

"Thanks, Cloyd. Uh, I figured just because they couldn't get enough gold out of here to keep workin' it, there might still be a few traces of the shiny stuff. Enough to keep me goin', anyway."

"Yeah? You find any?" Cloyd said with a cynical snort.

"Well, no, not yet. I just ain't found the right place," Devlin muttered humbly.

"Have you found anythin' at all?"

"No. Nothin' but a little copper ore, some rats, and a mess of spiders."

Cloyd considered what Devlin had said and wondered if his own assessment of this being the location of the money stash might be wrong.

"How long you been doin' this, Devlin?"

"About two weeks, almost every night. Missed the last three nights, though, because I had to stay late unloadin' barrels for the saloon. Too tired after that, you know."

That meant that Drago could have just missed running into Devlin. If the old man had been there when Drago came to hide the money, he'd have plugged Devlin without so much as a second thought. That money could still be here, thought Cloyd. But before he could look, he had to get rid of Devlin.

"Okay. Tell you what, Devlin," said Cloyd, "I'm going to help you look for your gold. But you got to promise me something, and that is you'll only come here when I'm with you."

"Why's that, Cloyd?"

"Because Sheriff Drago has said that if he catches anybody messin' around these old mines, he'll just up and string 'em up for poachin', that's why."

"How come it's poachin'?"

"Just because the mine is closed don't mean the owner don't still own it, and it's trespassin' or something like that if you get caught sneakin' around in here, and it's poachin' if you take anything out. That make sense to you?"

"Uh, yeah. I reckon I see what you're sayin', Cloyd."

"So, we got a deal? If we get caught, I'll just say we was checkin' to make sure nobody was doin' somethin' they shouldn't. Since I'm a deputy, I can make up stuff like that."

Devlin rubbed his chin for a few moments before nodding. "Okay, you got yourself a deal. I don't fancy gettin' my neck stretched for a few ounces of color."

Cloyd then convinced Devlin they'd stayed long enough, and it was time to turn in. They recovered their horses and went back to town. It was after midnight when Cloyd reached his little room and dropped into bed, secure in the belief that he'd be able to search the mine and have someone to cover his back should Drago show up.

Since there was no one else in the restaurant, Nettie asked if she could join Kelly. He lit up at the prospect of sharing her company and stood, pulling out a chair as she sat down with a cup of coffee in her hand.

"Mighty fine eats," said Kelly.

"Thank you. It's good to see a man enjoy his food." Nettie looked wistful as she stared at her cup. "You're new to the town of Cochise. Are you a businessman?" she said.

Kelly pulled back his black vest to show the silver badge pinned there.

"Oh, a lawman." She seemed to slump a bit as she said it.

"Did some lawman do something to make you dislike us?"

"Oh, it's not that I don't like you. It's just that none

of you stays in one place very long. Always traveling around, never able to settle down, getting shot at all the time."

"There's some truth to what you say. Is your husband a lawman?"

"My, uh, husband has been dead two years now. He was shot in the back by a, uh, man in Tombstone. I didn't have enough money to go back to Kansas, where I was brought up, so I moved here and talked the bank into lending me the money to open this place."

"And a fine place it is. I'm sorry about your husband."

"Thank you."

"You plannin' on going back to Kansas someday?"

"Maybe. I don't know. Business has been good, and I've been able to take care of myself pretty well. Sheriff Stevens seems capable of keeping things relatively quiet around here, so . . ."

"So, you're biding your time until . . . what?"

Nettie turned her head to look him straight in the eye, a question forming in her mind, a question without an answer. She settled for a shake of her head and a shrug. Nettie reminded him of the woman he'd loved and lost, a victim of the fever. He hadn't thought anyone could ever stir such desire in his soul again, yet now, as he looked into Nettie's eyes, he wasn't so sure.

Kelly returned to the jail to check on Spotted Dog and to make sure he'd been given something to eat. When the marshal opened the door, Jed was sitting at the sheriffs desk, eating.

"Evenin', Deputy. Just thought I would see if the Indian got his meal," said Kelly.

The deputy looked up and snorted. He was hunched over a plate of chicken and dumplings, stuffing food into his mouth as fast as he could.

"He weren't hungry. So I'm eatin' it for him," the deputy said, his mouth so full, his words were muffled.

Kelly's ire rose so fast that the deputy was caught completely off guard midbite. The marshal slammed the butt of his Winchester down in the middle of the feast, smashing the china, spilling coffee, and leaving a deep dent in the tray. The deputy's eyes became as large as the now-shattered saucer on which the cup of coffee had been sitting seconds before.

"Listen, you little weasel, you get over to the restaurant and get a new tray of food for the Indian. I'll be waiting right here. If you're not back in ten minutes, you'd better be on your way to Mexico. Now, git!"

The deputy thrust his hand out to grab the bowie knife that was lying on the desk beside a small pile of wood shavings, then clearly thought better of it and scrambled to his feet, nearly tripping over his own chair as he rushed out the door. Kelly grinned after him as he went back to see the Indian, who was sitting on the edge of the rough wooden bunk in a corner of the cell.

"How are you feeling, Spotted Dog?"

"I grow stronger by the hour."

"There is food on the way. After you've eaten, we'll talk. I have much to discuss with you."

Spotted Dog nodded his acceptance.

"Why am I kept a prisoner?" he said.

"It is to keep you safe. You won't be here long. The two of us will be leavin' as soon as you can travel," said Kelly.

Chapter Seven

The next morning, Kelly went to the sheriff's office to talk about the previous evening's confrontation.

"John Henry, we've been friends for quite a spell, but I can't abide a deputy who treats his prisoners badly," Kelly said. "I reckon you've heard about my interrupting his dinner."

"Yeah. Jed was the only man in town who was willing to take the deputy job. He's a poor excuse for a man, I'll admit, but I can't be here all the time. I'll get someone else as soon as I can."

"Fair enough. But I'd better not catch him doin' somethin' like that again. Anyway, I need to talk to you about a couple things. Got time for some breakfast?"

"Sure. Nothin's stirrin' that needs my attention," Stevens said.

"How about we go down to Miss Nettie's?"

"Fine."

As they entered the restaurant, Kelly was struck by the way Nettie's smile seemed to light up the whole room as she looked up from pouring coffee for a customer. White lace curtains hung at both front windows, barely able to hold back the intense sun but giving the place the feeling of home. Both men hung their hats on pegs on the wall next to the door. They shuffled across the room and took seats at a small table by a window.

"Good morning, gentlemen. Would you like coffee?"

"Sure. A couple of eggs and biscuits and gravy for me," said John Henry.

Kelly nodded that he'd have the same. After Nettie went back to the kitchen, Kelly leaned over to the sheriff to avoid having the other four people in the restaurant overhear what they were saying.

"Last night, Nettie said her husband had been shot in the back by someone in Tombstone. What do you know about that?"

"I only came here a year and a half ago, and she was already here. Whatever happened to her husband occurred before my time," the sheriff said.

The two stopped talking as Nettie came back with their breakfasts.

"Thank you, ma'am. This looks mighty appetizin'," said Kelly.

She lingered for a moment, then returned to her chores.

"She's a very striking woman. Yes, sir, very striking," mused Stevens. "And I notice it wasn't lost on you, either."

They both chuckled as they dug in.

"Since I've never seen your eyes light up like that around no other woman, I'll do some nosin' around on the matter . . . just as a favor to an ol' friend," said Stevens with a sly grin.

Kelly just nodded, as he had his mouth full.

Drago was in his usual foul mood when he stomped up the steps, pushed open the door to his office, and discovered Cloyd looking through his desk drawers.

Startled, Cloyd stood up quickly. "Uh, howdy, Sheriff. I, uh, was just looking for a dodger I thought I remembered seeing a couple days back. It, uh, was on some drifter named Texas Jack Boyle wanted for robbery. I-I think I may have seen him over to the saloon yesterday," stammered Cloyd.

"Uh-huh. You stupid oaf, you can't even tell a lie without foulin' it up. That Boyle fella got himself hanged a year ago. Now, what was you really doin' goin' through my papers?"

Drago shoved him aside and took his seat.

Cloyd hurriedly moved around the desk and swallowed hard before he spoke. "Okay. You remember that two dollars you lent me last month? And you wrote it down on a slip of paper? Well, to tell the truth, I ain't got the money, and I was lookin' to find that piece of paper and tear it up, hopin' you'd forgot," Cloyd said.

"Well, I haven't, and if I ever catch you going through my desk again, I'll flat out shoot you right through the gizzard. You got that?"

"Y-yes, sir. I got it plain. Won't never happen again," said Cloyd, wiping sweat off his brow. He hadn't been looking for any paper concerning money owed by him to the sheriff. He was looking to see if Drago had written down the whereabouts of the money they'd stolen, and it was his misfortune to get caught before he could find anything. His hastily made-up story seemed to have satisfied the sheriff—for now, at least. He let out a low sigh and eased into a chair across the desk from Drago.

The sheriff began leafing through dodgers on wanted men that formed a small pile in his desk drawer. He wadded up a couple that were for men he knew were dead and tossed them to the floor. But Cloyd had reminded him of something. That something could net him a few extra dollars and get rid of his bumbling fool deputy once and for all.

After breakfast, Kelly walked back to the jail with Sheriff Stevens. He wanted to talk to Spotted Dog about the charges the sheriff sought to bring against him. Kelly needed to hear the Indian's story firsthand, before some hotheaded citizens decided it was their duty to rid the county of one more Apache.

"I'm goin' back to talk to the Indian, John Henry."

"Sure, sure. Take your time. I need some ammunition, anyway, so I'm goin' down to the hardware store to buy a couple boxes. I'll be back soon. Reckon you can watch the store for me," the sheriff said with a snicker.

After Stevens left, Kelly went back to the cell, where Spotted Dog was lying on the bunk. He struggled to sit up at the sound of Kelly's boots creaking on the wooden floor.

"How are you feelin' today, Spotted Dog?"

"I grow stronger with each passing of the sun."

"Good. I'd like to take you out of here soon and get to the bottom of these stories I hear about you."

"You hear words about me?"

"They're sayin' you were with some men who robbed a stagecoach, then shot and killed the driver and the guard and two passengers. They say it happened not far from here and that you were shot by a sheriff who tracked the five of you to a place where they found you hidin'."

Spotted Dog just stared at Kelly in amazement at the words he was hearing. He hung his head and groaned.

"It is bad that my people want me dead, but now your people also. You should have let me die quietly on the hot sands where you found me. I would be better off."

"I haven't said I believe them. I have many questions that need answers before I let anythin' happen to you. You are safe with me, but you must be honest and tell me everythin' you know about the incident," said Kelly.

"I know nothing of which you speak. It is like telling about an eagle I have never seen."

"Okay, maybe your bein' shot and fallin' into that ravine you told me about caused you to forget things. We'll talk about those things you do know, and maybe you'll remember something useful."

"I only remember what happened to me that day. We left our village to search for food. The wagons carrying meat from the Indian Agent had not arrived for many days, and my people were growing hungry and restless. To keep more trouble from visiting my people, five of us were sent out to bring back fresh meat. When we came to a small canyon, we saw tracks of deer. There were several of them. I was sent to the top of a rise to see if I could see them nearby."

"So that's when you climbed up to where you were shot?"

"As I reach the top, I am knocked off my feet and roll down the hill into a mesquite bush. As I stand up, I re-alize I was shot. Then I know why they send me to look for the deer; it was so they could kill me as I climbed. I heard many shots at the same time I was hit. They weren't as good with the rifles as they thought," said Spotted Dog. He stared at the wall, shaking his head.

"Did you see any other men, white men?"

"I saw no others."

"Do you think you could find that place again?"

Spotted Dog frowned, then began nodding. "I can find the place. Do we go now?"

"Not just yet. You need to get more of your strength back, and I need to tend to a couple things. I'll return later."

Spotted Dog was still sitting on the edge of the bunk when Kelly let the steel-barred door close behind him. The sound of the lock's falling into place scared the old Indian. He didn't like feeling like a prisoner.

Flower Drago was tired of sitting around the hot, cramped cabin and was considering a little getaway from Liberty and her abusive husband. Maybe she'd take the stage to the next town and look up an old friend.

Flower wasn't confident that Emmett would let her go, even if she promised to return after a few days. He was very possessive, and the slightest hint of her wandering away from him, even for a short time, could set him off on an angry tirade, a fit of jealousy over the chance that she might meet up with someone more sympathetic to her needs. His fits of anger almost always guaranteed that she'd be staying indoors for the week or so it took for the black-and-blue marks on her face to go away. Emmett made it clear he saw nothing unmanly in keeping a woman in line, especially one with a smart mouth.

She decided she'd gather up her things and pack them in a large carpetbag her aunt had given her years ago. She put a few items into the bag and shoved it under their bed, where she hoped her husband wouldn't notice it until she could get onto the stagecoach headed to Cochise. Actually, she couldn't really explain even to herself why she had stayed with him so long, getting slapped around so often, it had almost become predictable. She would sometimes lie in bed and pray someone would come to town who was better with a revolver than Emmett Drago, who would shoot him down in the street.

Flower and Emmett hadn't been church married, just said a few words in front of a drunken circuit judge in the saloon where she worked—no signed paper or anything. Yet she'd clung tenaciously to her hopes and dreams that finally she'd found a way out of the dead-end life of a saloon girl, dancing with cowboys and getting them to buy more drinks. Now she wondered why she kept making the same stupid mistakes again and again. And she prayed some more.

Drago sent Cloyd off to check out the saloon and make sure no miners or cowboys were getting too rowdy. As soon as the deputy left, Drago pulled out the folded wanted poster with all the particulars on a man wanted for rustling cattle. There was mention of a possible killing too. But, to the greedy sheriff, it didn't matter how many crimes the fella had committed, just that he was wanted and there was a reward for him. Drago grinned as he stared at the yellowing paper. The likeness of Cloyd was excellent.

Chapter Eight

K elly was awakened in the middle of the night by gunshots and yelling. Pulling on his pants and boots, he grabbed his Winchester and ran to see what was going on. As he reached the door, a bullet shattered one of the front windows of the hotel. He ducked back inside for a moment. He checked to make sure he'd chambered a round, then took a quick peek out the gaping hole ringed with broken glass in what was left of the window frame to get his bearings.

Gunfire was originating from what appeared to be several sources across the street and down an alley. The shooters were on either side of the jail, keeping well back in the shadows so they couldn't be identified. And they didn't appear to be shooting at anyone in particular either, more firing off covering shots to keep people from running out into the street. Suddenly the door to the jail burst open, and two figures ran from the building, half dragging, half carrying a third figure. That figure, Kelly guessed, was Spotted Dog.

The gunfire stopped as soon as the three disappeared into the darkness. The next thing Kelly heard was the pounding of hooves heading out of town fast. He ran across the street to see if the sheriff was okay. What he found was the deputy, lying on the floor, out cold.

Kelly rushed to the cells to confirm his suspicions. Indeed, the cell was open, and the Indian was gone. Just then Sheriff Stevens burst through the open door.

"What happened? I heard shots and came as fast as I could, but . . . Oh, no! Who did this, Marshal?"

"I don't know. I just got here myself. The Indian is gone. Either some citizens had it in mind not to wait for a judge and jury, or Spotted Dog's people didn't like his being incarcerated. Either way, we won't know until we go after them."

"We'll not find much of a trail in the dark. Might as well wait until dawn; then I'll get a posse together," said Stevens. He stared down at the deputy, who was just coming around and shaking his head. Jed leaned against the desk for support, as he was weak from getting hit over the head. A large knot was forming on his scalp.

"Deputy, did you see who did this?" said Kelly.

"I, uh, was asleep when something hit me. I didn't get a look at 'em," said the deputy. He was blinking, trying to focus his eyes. "I'm kinda dizzy. Am I shot or anything?"

"No, you're not shot," said John Henry. "But if you weren't sleepin' on the job, maybe you'd have been able to stop whoever it was from takin' the prisoner. You are worthless."

The deputy just moaned and rocked back and forth, propped up against the desk.

"I'm sorry, Marshal. I know I said he wasn't much of a deputy. I reckon this proves it."

"Do you want to stay here and tend to him?"

"No. I'll be ready to ride at dawn. Don't you worry 'bout that."

Kelly turned and left the sheriff alone to solve his own problem. He walked back to his room through the throng of onlookers who had gathered outside the sheriff's office.

"Everything all right in there, mister?" someone said as Kelly walked past.

"Better find a doctor. Man in there's got a nasty bump on the head," said Kelly, and he kept on moving with no further word of explanation.

When Drago got home that evening, he had been drinking more than usual. His mood was bad, and he didn't want to listen to Flower's questions about his whereabouts. He just stormed in and threw himself into a chair at the kitchen table, weaving a little to keep his unsteady balance.

"Get me somethin' to eat, woman, and be quick about it. I ain't lookin' for none of your sass, neither." Drago began yelling the second he entered the house.

Flower, who had been asleep, was shaken by his belligerence. She hastily threw on a robe over her nightdress and was tying the belt around her as she left the bedroom and entered the cabin's main room. She was nervous about what she had been planning and couldn't take any chances he'd find out, especially when he was drunk. She carefully stepped into the kitchen and began cutting some bread and a piece of pork to fry. She stoked the stove to get a flame, then added some kindling. It wouldn't take long to get the stove hot enough to cook on, but whatever time it took was bound to be too much for a man like Emmett Drago, a man with a very short fuse.

She said, "I'll get you a cool drink of water and fetch some eggs from the back porch. It won't take a minute to whip something up. You just rest awhile, honey," she said nervously.

Drago sensed her meekness, and he didn't like it, didn't like that whiny tone that Flower sometimes took on. Whenever she was like this—to his mind, at least—she was up to something. And that made him even more violent. As she started to get the eggs, he rose out of his chair and stumbled toward her, grabbing at her sleeve and yanking her toward him.

"What are you up to?" he said. His breath reeked of whiskey. It almost gagged her. "Somethin's goin' on here. I can feel it."

She tried to break his grip but to no avail. "Nothin' is goin' on, Drago. Nothin'. Why would you think there is?"

"I can tell when you're lyin', Flower. Now, out with it. I got no time for your foolishness!"

Without warning, he struck her hard across the mouth with the back of one hand. She fell backward against the cupboard, then slipped to the floor, tearing her robe as it caught on the edge of the table. She struggled to stand but knew it was hopeless; he would just knock her down again, so she sat there on the floor and burst into tears.

"There's no use tryin' them tears on me. It's been tried before. I'm too smart to fall for them women's ways!" he shouted, then raised his arm to hit her again. But by then the whiskey had gained full control of him, and as his eyes rolled up in his head, he fell backward, landing flat on his back with a crash in the middle of the floor, out cold. Flower left him right where he fell and returned to bed to finalize her plan to escape from her tormentor. He didn't awaken until after dawn.

That next morning, Flower planned to act as if nothing had happened, except that she couldn't do much to cover the dark mark on her cheek and the cut on her lip where Emmett had hit her. As she crawled from beneath her covers and shuffled into the kitchen, she found him sitting at the table, holding his head and moaning.

She went to the stove to heat up some coffee. She said nothing to him but hummed softly to herself.

"I'll have some of that coffee. And make me some eggs while you're at it," he mumbled, his eyes closed to avoid the bright sunlight sneaking in through the window over the washbasin.

"Okay," she said.

"I reckon I must have passed out last night. I was on the floor this mornin' when I woke. Did I say anything when I came in?"

She placed some coffee in front of him. That was the first time he saw her face—the bruise and the cut on her lip.

"Oh. Did I do that?" he said in a soft tone.

"Yes. But you didn't know what you were doin'. You was just drunk." Flower turned away to put some pork slices into a skillet. A loaf of bread sat on the sideboard, several slices already cut from the night before.

"I say anything?" he said again.

"Just accused me of somethin' I couldn't make heads or tails of," she said.

He took a sip of coffee as he pondered what to say next. He figured he had to have been pretty angry to hit her like that. But then, it seemed he was always angry at her for something or another. She was still a beautiful woman, and he couldn't quite put his finger on what it was about her that made him so furious. For the life of him, he couldn't figure it out. When he'd brought her to Liberty, he had every intention of seeing the two of them all nice and cozy in their little bungalow, of living a simple, happy life; but somewhere along the way a devil got inside him and twisted him all up. He couldn't seem to control his temper once it washed up to the surface. And, of course, he was pretty sure liquor was not his friend. Maybe that was his devil, he thought.

If he had asked Flower, she would have been happy to tell him what the problem was: He was just a mean, crazy drunk. Plain and simple.

After he finished eating, he washed his face in the basin, finger-combed his hair, and put his bowler hat back on after straightening the large dent in the crown caused by falling flat on his back the night before. He mumbled something about getting over to the jail, and he wobbled out the door, leaving it wide open, whistling as if nothing had happened.

When he disappeared from view, Flower hurried into the bedroom to get dressed. She could afford to wait no longer to go to the stage office to buy a ticket for Cochise with the money she'd saved up from the meager allowance Emmett gave her each week for food. She would go the back way, so she couldn't be seen from the sheriff's office or the saloon, whichever place Emmett actually inhabited during the day. She wasn't entirely certain.

As she entered the stage office, she looked around to see if there was anyone she knew hanging around. There wasn't, so she went to the window and asked the ticket manager for a schedule of stagecoaches to Cochise and how much it cost to get there.

"One way or comin' back?" he asked.

Flower thought on that for a minute, then said, "I reckon one way. That way I can come back on my own schedule." She plunked down the dollar and twenty-five cents for the fare, stuffed her ticket into her handbag, and turned to leave.

"Best be here a few minutes early, miss," the ticket manager said. "Leaves promptly at nine-thirty."

Flower smiled at him as she started for the door. But just as she reached for the handle, the door opened, and in came Cloyd.

He tipped his hat to her. "Top o' the day, Miz Drago," he said. "Goin' on a trip?"

Flower was too shaken to even acknowledge his presence. She pushed by him, hurried out the door, and ran down the back alley all the way home. Tears began to run down her cheeks as she cursed herself for getting into this mess in the first place.

Chapter Nine

Kelly met Sheriff Stevens and four other men in front of the jail just before dawn. The sheriff stood on the steps, swearing in some of the local citizenry who had volunteered to join the posse. The locals were understandably eager for answers as to who had robbed the stagecoach, and they might not shy away from a little rope justice if they thought they had the shooter. But to Kelly, none of them looked like anything other than what they were: a storekeeper, the liveryman, a part-time bartender, and the blacksmith. No gunmen, no hard cases. For that, Kelly was grateful, because he had a feeling he could have problems when they caught up to whoever had taken Spotted Dog, and he didn't favor having to deal with gunslingers wanting to gain a modicum of celebrity for helping capture the ones who raided the jail and stole a prisoner. At the moment, based solely on the word of the sheriff in Liberty, the Indian was the only suspect they had. And now even he was missing. That didn't sit well with a number of the residents, including Sheriff John Henry Stevens. In fact, at that very moment, Kelly might have been the only friend Spotted Dog had.

"Are you all armed? Got plenty of ammunition?" John Henry asked. Everyone nodded yes. "Okay, then, let's ride."

"Where's your deputy, John Henry?" asked Kelly.

"That fool ain't good for nothin' but watchin' the store since he got liquored up a few days back, dropped his own gun, and shot himself in the shoulder. That was after he'd been gone for two days, probably carousing over in Liberty," said Stevens. "Leastways that was his excuse."

Kelly just shook his head as he eyed the firepower that was spread among them, mostly pistols of varying sizes and two rifles, one of them a big Sharps .50 buffalo gun. That was the one to keep an eye on, with its .50-caliber bullet able to strike an object several hundred yards away. The Sharps belonged to the blacksmith, a bulky man with large arms and a quiet manner. But then, Kelly was well aware that manners could be deceiving.

The six of them mounted up and began their trek into the desert southeast of town. That's where the trail led them, although Kelly wasn't certain just how reliable that trail would be, since whoever took the Indian had to know they would be pursued. Leaving an obvious trail wasn't smart unless it was a false trail or there was a surprise awaiting anyone who came too close.

"Got any ideas about who we might be after, Marshal?" said Stevens.

"Well, it wasn't any of the townsfolk, that's for certain. You've probably noticed that the horses we're following aren't shod."

By noon, the trail was becoming more difficult to follow as it rose into foothills covered with varying types of cacti, many of which appeared quite lethal, then narrowed among building-size boulders that began to dot the landscape everywhere. As the ground changed from dirt to gravel to shale and then to almost solid rock, hoofprints that were previously clear and easy to follow were now becoming only vague hints that a horse had recently passed. Kelly could see that soon all trace of riders would be difficult to read, if not impossible to follow, and the posse might as well turn back. The people they were trying to track knew what they were doing, forcing their pursuers into inhospitable and unfamiliar terrain, full of switchbacks and box canyons. And since they'd taken Spotted Dog, and their ponies were unshod, Indians were most certainly the abductors. That would make the whole situation much more difficult. For all Kelly knew, the two lawmen and the four citizens newly sworn to act as a posse might be only minutes away from riding into an ambush. And those four townsfolk were rank amateurs.

"Let's hold up here a minute, John Henry," said Kelly. "The trail's gettin' cold, and I'm not sure we should take inexperienced men into such hostile territory. We don't know what lies ahead, and with only six of us, things could get mighty rough. From the looks of where we're bein' led, I'd say it's certain we're chasin' a bunch of Apaches."

Stevens reined in and sat with his hands crossed on the pommel of his saddle. He removed his hat, wiped the perspiration off his brow, then replaced the old, faded, floppy-brimmed hat he'd worn for ten years. "I think you're right, but I don't like the idea of givin' up on those varmints after no more'n a day's ride."

"I understand your misgivin's, John Henry, but for all we know, we're chasin' a band of Chiricahuas who have nothin' to lose by leadin' us into an ambush."

John Henry thought for a moment before coming to the same conclusion. "I reckon you got a point there. I admit I've been gettin' a little uneasy myself. The trail's all but petered out, anyway. I 'spect we might as well head back."

Stevens turned in his saddle and signaled for the others to start back the way they had come.

"I'm willing to go on," said the blacksmith. "We'll come upon them sooner or later, don't you think?"

"I'm in no position to know what we might run into in them mountains. Plenty of those red devils up there, and I don't aim to offer them an easy target. Kelly's right: We'd best head back and live to fight another day."

Grumbling could be heard within the ranks, but all the men wheeled their mounts around and began slowly retracing their own trail. All, that is, but Kelly. The marshal sat staring off into the distance for a minute, lost in thought.

It wasn't until they were almost out of sight that Stevens noticed the marshal wasn't with them. He stopped, told the others he'd catch up, and returned to where he'd left Kelly.

"What's goin' through your mind, Marshal? Thought we'd decided to turn back."

"You'll probably think this odd, but I'd like to find out just what those Indians are up to."

"I don't get your drift. Seems clear to me that all they want is to free one of their own."

"That's just it. Spotted Dog said he was shot in the back by his own people. If that were true, why bother to free him? Why not let the white man hang him and be done with it—that is, if all they want is to see him dead."

"You certain he didn't shoot himself to make it look like an ambush and give himself an alibi?"

"Shoot himself in the back?"

The sheriff frowned at the impracticality of his own remark, removed his hat once again, wiped his brow with a handkerchief, and resettled himself in the saddle, as Kelly continued.

"I think there's more to it. I doubt the Indians are in favor of us handin' out our justice for them. They've had more than their share of that already."

"So what you're sayin' is that if there's a killin' to be done, they want the bullet to come from one of their own?" said John Henry.

"I suppose it could come down to that, but there's another possibility. What if he wasn't shot by his own people in the first place?" said Kelly.

"Who else?"

"That's what I aim to find out."

"How do you plan on goin' about that?"

"Send the others on back to town. You and I will make camp over there on the top of that bluff. Plenty of cover if we are attacked, but also an easy place to parlay if they were of a mind to do so," said Kelly. "We'll see if they'll come to us."

"And if you're wrong, and they're dead set on eliminatin' two lawmen?"

"Got your will made out?" Kelly said with a grin.

John Henry just sighed and rode ahead to tell the other four to continue on back to town without them. He wasn't all that confident that Kelly's plan would work, but then, he didn't have one of his own. He hadn't liked abandoning the pursuit of Spotted Dog in the first place. The marshal's plan did seem a means to find out which way the wind blew in the matter. If Spotted Dog's people wanted him dead, they could easily just go ahead and shoot him now, then return to the reservation. If they could see that the posse had broken up, and they wanted to strike a deal to keep the law off their backs in the future for their actions in freeing one of their own, this would be their opportunity. If they returned to the reservation, taking the prisoner with them, it would be pretty easy for a troop of cavalry to ride in, take Spotted Dog, and extract a little payback for their bold raid on the jail in Cochise. Trying to talk a couple of lawmen out of such recompense would be a smart move.

When Stevens returned, he and the marshal turned their mounts north to the small bluff. The location would give them a good view of the surrounding landscape yet not look like a fortress set up by two men, at least one of whom was well known for his abilities with a rifle. They dismounted, found a place where their hobbled horses would be hard to steal in the middle of the night, then set about building a small campfire to heat coffee and some beans.

"We want to make it obvious we're no longer on their trail, that we've given up the pursuit," said Kelly. "I hope they take the bait."

"Do you really think they'll fall for such a bluff?" said Stevens.

"We'll be ready for whatever they plan. One way or another, before this night is out, I hope to know what's become of Spotted Dog."

While Kelly had put considerable thought into the idea, he had to admit he never quite understood how an Indian reasoned. That could, as he was well aware, end up being his undoing.

Flower Drago sat by the window in the kitchen, fearing the moment her husband would come through that door. She knew Cloyd couldn't keep his mouth shut, and as soon as Emmett got wind of her being at the stage office, he'd get some liquor into him, then come busting in, roaring drunk, and commence to beat her silly. She shook at the prospect of another beating, another in a long line of being slapped around she could no longer take but couldn't seem to avoid, no matter what attitude she struck. She hung her head and prayed for something to happen to him, for someone to draw on him and come up the winner, or for his horse to shy and throw him onto his head in the street, maybe break his neck—anything to keep him away from her.

Just then she heard footsteps on the porch. The latch turned, and she looked up to see Cloyd standing in the doorway, wearing an evil smirk. He removed his hat and came in, uninvited, bold as you please. Flower knew he had something on his mind, and she was pretty sure she wasn't going to like it.

"Howdy, Miz Flower," he said. "You're lookin' mighty pretty today. I couldn't help but notice how them blue eyes of yours were like shiny gemstones when I saw you at the stage depot."

Flower just stared at him in disbelief that he'd have the courage to walk into the sheriff's house without even a howdy-do. She swallowed hard as she tried to decide what to do next. Cloyd was as mean as a snake, and he wasn't the type to pass out compliments like licorice candy. And he could forget being a ladies' man, because he was coarse, homely, and filthy. But he hadn't come here without some purpose, and Flower had a sick feeling she knew exactly what that purpose was—a purpose she had fought off before. She didn't have to wait long to find out, either.

"Miz Flower, I figured you was fixin' to take off and leave poor ol' Sheriff Drago to do his own cookin'. So, I says to myself, what should I, a dutiful deputy, do? Should I run and tell the man his wife is going away, or should I keep my mouth shut? And what would be a proper reward for such a kindly act?"

"And you are wondering just how grateful I'd be, right?"

"Why, Miz Flower, you done took the words right outta my mouth."

Chapter Ten

As the evening shadows lengthened, and the sun began to slip behind the western range, Kelly and John Henry talked across the crackling fire, reminiscing about the days when they served as lawmen in some of the cattle towns in Kansas—Dodge City, Ellsworth, and Abilene—and about the people they'd known, many of whom were no longer alive.

"Were you around when Sheriff C. B. Whitney got himself gunned down by that crazy drunk Billy Thompson up in Ellsworth back in seventy-three? Hit him full with a blast from his brother Ben's double-barreled shotgun," Stevens said, lighting a pipe and settling down against his saddle.

"No. I heard about it, though. Never knew Whitney, but I heard he was a decent sort," said Kelly. "I heard Billy claimed it was an accident."

"Why, even Billy's brother, Ben, didn't buy that story. He had to hold off the town to let Billy escape; otherwise, he'd likely have been hangin' from a nearby telegraph pole. Even though he was hurtin' real bad, the old sheriff himself claimed it was unintentional. But I'll tell you, whenever Billy'd get all liquored up, he could be meaner than a snake and like as not to strike at any moment."

"So, are you sayin' it might have been on purpose?"

"Don't reckon we'll ever know."

"I recollect that the Ellsworth police were a pretty questionable bunch around that time. Any truth to that?" said Kelly. "You never were a part of that, were you?"

"Nope. I was a deputy over in Abilene for a spell, but I never spent much time in Ellsworth," said Stevens. "But the stories that came out of those cattle towns back then were enough to curl your hair."

"I was still in Dodge when that bunch of buffalo hunters went down to Texas to see who could bag the biggest number of those shaggy beasts. I remember they got themselves tangled up with a bunch of Kiowa, Cheyenne, and Comanche at a place called Adobe Walls in seventy-four," said Kelly.

"Yeah, I remember. Wasn't that where some fella dropped one of them redskins off his horse with some sort of a miracle shot?"

"Yep. Billy Dixon knocked a redskin clean off his saddle from over fifteen hundred yards. Didn't kill him, though, just bruised him a bit. Some of them measured that shot later. A fine piece of shootin'," said Kelly. "Masterful. The Indians skedaddled after that."

"What was it that made you decide to become a lawman, Kelly?"

"Almost didn't. My father was a minister. I was expected to follow in his footsteps. I would have too, but he was gunned down by a couple of men who were trying to rob the bank in the little town in Kansas where I grew up."

"Why'd they shoot a minister? He wouldn't have done them any harm."

"He stepped in between one of the robbers and a woman who had refused to part with her money. The shooter warned him to step aside, but my father told him he was here on earth to do the Lord's work, and part of that was to protect the innocent."

"And they shot him, anyway?"

"Yep, but the lady was unharmed. That was the day I decided I could follow in my father's footsteps but in a different way. I figured to protect the innocent from behind a badge."

"Ever regret doin' it?" said Stevens.

"Nope. I carry a little book of verse with me wherever I go, just in case I'm tempted to wander off that very narrow path."

"And . . . ?"

"And it's never failed me. Besides, it's real good readin' on a lonely night."

As they continued to exchange remembrances, the sun disappeared below the horizon, and only a slight pink glow remained. They seemed to have talked for hours about old times and shared stories that neither ever got tired of hearing.

But for all their patient waiting, nothing was happening to make them believe the Indians were going to take the bait. Disappointed, Kelly scooted down on his blanket, settled in with his head propped against his saddle, pulled his cavalry-style Stetson down over his eyes, and drifted off to sleep. Stevens wasn't far behind, taking a couple of final drags on his pipe, then adding a few more sticks to the fire to ward off the night chill before he, too, settled down for the night. The sounds of night creatures surrounded them like a mother's lullaby. Soon both were gone to the world, oblivious of their surroundings and any danger that might be lurking there.

But as the sun broke in the east, a surprise awaited them as they began to stir under their blankets. Kelly, suddenly cognizant of someone watching him, sat straight up, grabbing his Winchester carbine as he did. He blinked at what he saw, uncertain if he might be dreaming. Then it became clear that he was wide awake, for there in front of him, sitting casually on his haunches on the other side of the fire pit, was Spotted Dog. Behind him, several feet away, were four armed Apaches.

"John Henry, wake up. You aren't going to believe this," said Kelly.

"I-I'm awake. Uh, wh-what is it?" He struggled to free himself from his blanket as his eyes began to focus on the subject of Kelly's concern. "Well, I'll be."

"Spotted Dog, what are you doin' here?" asked Kelly.

"Come to help you find killers."

"These the friends who took you from the jail?"

"Some of my people. Scouts I was with for many moons. They did not understand that I was not a prisoner but your friend."

"Who-ee, Injun, you sure do make it hard to figure where you stand in all this," mumbled Stevens. "How many of your friends helped you escape?"

"Five more. They have gone back to our people. They will not return."

"Are you sayin' you want to help me find the men who robbed the stage and killed four people? Do you have any knowledge of who they might be?" Kelly asked.

"No, but my brothers are good trackers, can be of great help. Will we get paid?" Spotted Dog grinned at the surprised expression that formed on Kelly's face as he was asked for a job.

Stevens wore a smirk as he looked over at the marshal and said, "I didn't know you were lookin' to hire on deputies, Kelly. Shoulda put a notice in the newspaper."

The four Apaches who accompanied Spotted Dog were well armed; each carried a Spencer rifle decorated with brass tacks in different designs on the stock. The Indians were obviously scouts, or former scouts, probably originally enlisted by Indian Agent John Clum before he left the San Carlos reservation in '77. They held their rifles at their sides, barrels pointing at the ground, suggesting no belligerent intent. The four remained silent, patient.

Kelly looked at Stevens for a moment before turning back to the Indian who sat across the now-cold ashes of the fire pit. He had mixed emotions about bringing Spotted Dog formally into the investigation of the stagecoach robbery and killings and the murder of George Alvord. He was used to working alone and had from experience learned the downside to including civilians in anything that could possibly involve gunplay. Perhaps Spotted Dog could be helpful, but Kelly wasn't firmly convinced. He needed to remain cautious if optimistic.

"All right, Spotted Dog, I'll let you come along for the time being, anyway, if you'll take me to the spot where you were shot. After that, I can't promise I'll have any need for you and your friends."

"You will give us food?"

"Build up that fire, and we'll make some coffee and share what provisions we have with you."

"I will do as you ask."

Flower was terrified at the prospect of Cloyd's laying a hand on her. Her hatred of the man was fierce, and nothing short of her being dead would ever convince her to succumb to his advances without using every ounce of her strength to fight him off. He was larger than she was, but the fire of loathing burned hot inside her, giving her extra strength and a confidence that she could somehow at least make him sorry he'd ever come through that door.

Cloyd stood staring at Flower, grinning his licentious

grin, biding his time. He figured she would soon realize that there were worse things that could happen to her, such as Drago's finding out she was getting ready to take a trip, a trip he was certain the sheriff had no knowledge of. In fact, he was counting heavily on Drago's ignorance in the matter. He took a step toward her.

Flower took one step back and found that she was backed into a corner with only a shelf full of pans, utensils, and a water bucket on one side, a cabinet full of dishes on the other. She surreptitiously played her hands across the shelf, hoping to find a knife or a bottle— anything that could become a defensive weapon. If only she hadn't already cleaned up the kitchen and put things away; all the utensils were now out of reach. She spotted a drawer she hadn't completely closed. There were several knives in that drawer, but it was on the other side of the room, and Cloyd was between her and any chance of reaching it before he overcame her. Panic rose up in her throat like sickening bile. Her skin was moist, and her hands shook as if she had a palsy.

"Cloyd, you're making a big mistake here. If Emmett finds out what you're up to, you won't live long enough to make out your will. He'll skin you alive and cut you into little pieces. And I'll be there to cheer him on. Think hard on this thing. Think real hard," Flower said, struggling to get the words out without letting him see her trembling hands and how she was about to collapse from the fear that tightened around her like a hangman's noose.

"Why, Miz Flower, ol' Cloyd don't mean you no

harm. All I want is a chance for you and me to get to know each other a little better. It ain't like you never looked at no other man before Drago back when you was dancin' in that saloon in Tombstone."

"I wasn't married then, neither."

"Aw, shucks, what's a little ol' piece of paper mean, anyhow? Fact is, I ain't so sure you and the sheriff really are hitched, what I hear. And if that's so, then you're still just as unmarried as you were then, and you shouldn't be actin' so high-and-mighty. C'mon, you'll find me easy to please." He moved one step closer.

She could smell his rancid breath on her face. She nearly gagged.

Just then they heard footsteps on the front porch, seconds before Emmett Drago opened the door and caught Cloyd a mere three feet from his wife, who was cowering in a corner of the kitchen.

"Cloyd! What the devil are you doin' in my house? And why do you have my wife backed into a corner?" Drago pulled his revolver from its holster and cocked it, pointing it straight at Cloyd's head.

"Now, hold on, Drago. I ain't done nothin' but talk to Miz Flower. Ain't what you're a'thinkin'. I was just passin' by, seen she was—uh—sweepin' the porch, and I, uh, figured to stop by and, uh, see if there was anythin' she might need help with. Th-that's all. Ain't that right, Miz Flower?"

Flower could see the problem with denying Cloyd's claim. He might blurt out what he'd seen at the stage office, and then she'd be in for it. But if she supported his claim, he might be smart enough to keep his mouth shut. It was a big gamble to take either way, but one in which she had little choice.

"Sure. That's all it was, Emmett. I reckon Cloyd just wanted to be helpful."

Chapter Eleven

After Kelly, Stevens, and the five Indians had finished eating what provisions he'd brought, Kelly ordered them all to get ready to ride. He told Spotted Dog to lead the way, since he was the only one who knew the exact location where his shooting had taken place. Kelly's reservations at accompanying a superior number of armed Apache scouts into unknown territory kept him on high alert. With all the problems that had transpired between the Apaches and the white man in the Arizona Territory, he couldn't be faulted for having questions about this group. Why were they off the reservation? Spotted Dog said they had been sent out to look for food, but that didn't really ring quite true to a naturally suspicious marshal. But then, always ready to hear a man out before making a judgment, Kelly decided to wait and watch, staying ever mindful of the potential danger that lay with these fierce fighters and the fire-power that accompanied them. His hand remained close to his Colt revolver.

The Indians led the way, with Kelly and Stevens bringing up the rear of the column. Stevens had fallen back alongside the marshal so he could talk without being heard. Neither one knew how much of the white man's language the Indians understood, but since they were scouts, probably most of it.

"Got any idea where they're takin' us?" the sheriff said.

"None, except that I assume it's near where the stagecoach was robbed. Since you told me Sheriff Drago said he followed the Indians' tracks into the foothills before getting into a battle with them, they probably weren't too far away from where the crime took place. If the Indians did it, they must have felt fairly safe in deciding what to do with the spoils of their attack without having to wander too far. Of course, if, as Spotted Dog claims, they had nothin' to do with the robbery, they could have been innocent victims of mistaken identity," said Kelly.

"If they ain't guilty, and, mind you, I ain't making no judgments here, what put Drago onto their trail in the first place?"

"That's a good question. One we've got to get answered."

Into the late afternoon, they rode single file through the dusty desert, feeling their way among the cacti, mesquite, ocotillo, and brittlebush. A coyote dashed from behind some brush to cross their trail and disappear over a hillock. Birds fluttered uneasily nearby before flying off and settling down again farther away from the column, assuring themselves a safe distance from potential danger. Kelly had some of the same misgivings about his companions. Not certain what these Apache scouts were really after and what their intentions were when they found it, the marshal just stroked his mustache and kept an eye out for any hint of what might be coming. His Winchester had a cartridge already chambered, so he would only have to cock it to let that lethal weapon spit its deadly fire at any who might threaten his security. While he was never without his Colt revolver strapped around his waist, the Winchester was his weapon of choice for its accuracy at a distance. He seldom ever drew his Colt, but woe to the man who assumed he couldn't use it when necessary.

"From the description Drago gave of the robbery, I'd say it was down there somewhere, along that crooked stretch of trail," Stevens said, pointing across the arid land to where a road of sorts had been etched out of the desert by the repeated passing of stagecoaches and wagons.

Kelly watched to see if Spotted Dog even looked in the direction of where Stevens had whispered that the robbery might have taken place but saw no such recognition on the Indian's face. In fact, all Kelly saw was a weary old man who just wanted to be left alone to live out his days in peace.

"I don't claim to understand these people, John Henry, but I'm having a hard time seeing Spotted Dog as a stage robber."

"I know what you mean. But then, they say Billy the Kid looks like some dimwit who couldn't *load* a gun, let alone shoot someone with it," said Stevens.

"Just keep your eyes open. I have a feelin' we're goin' to get some answers soon."

He had no sooner spoken than Spotted Dog pointed to an area at the foot of a mountain that was thick with trees and boulders, cut through the middle by a deep ravine—a good place to hide if someone was of a mind to do just that. The seven of them continued in the direction that Spotted Dog said they should go. They arrived at the edge of the ravine about two hours later, just before sundown.

"Spotted Dog, how much farther?"

"Not far, only a short way to the bottom, and by the time the moon is up, we will find the camp we made that day."

"I don't want to be wanderin' around down there in the dark. We'll camp here for the night. Get a fresh start in the mornin'," said Kelly.

Spotted Dog just grunted, made a few gestures to the others, and dismounted. The Indians made their own camp several yards away from the two lawmen. Two fires were built. Two of the Indians went to hunt for their evening meal. As Kelly also started to go hunting, Spotted Dog told him the scouts would be back soon, and they would be returning with enough meat for all.

Kelly just shrugged, unwilling to put up an argument with a man who offered to bring back food without his having to make any effort at searching it out himself. In fact, it sounded like a pretty good arrangement.

As he awaited the Indians' return, Kelly sat by the fire he and Stevens had started and thought back on the last three days. His first thoughts were about Nettie and the way she had affected him, how he'd tossed and turned that first night after he met her. Something in the way she looked at him with those haunting blue eyes made a powerful impression, more so than any other woman since the loss of his wife, Katherine, to a fever. He struggled with a weighty conflict: putting his wife's memory aside enough to know how to deal with a beautiful woman who was obviously still trying to come to grips with the untimely death of her own husband. He was torn between the past and the present.

He had asked around town about the incident in which Nettie's husband had died, but no one seemed to know, although most said they hadn't really known Nettie very long and that it could have happened before their time. The one old-timer he'd asked appeared to have some problems remembering what he'd eaten that morning. Kelly decided his best way to get information would be to check with the newspaper editor when they got back to town. Although, he couldn't remember seeing a newspaper office in town.

"Get out of here, Cloyd, before I blow the top of your head clean off. And don't you ever come here again without an engraved invitation, which I guarantee you'll never get—do you understand?" Drago shouted through clenched teeth. "If I ever find you near my wife again, your ugly face won't be worth trying to identify!"

Drago put two quick shots into the floor just to make sure the deputy hadn't mistaken anything he'd said.

Cloyd nearly fell over his own feet trying to escape the house before Drago changed his mind about shooting him. He had seen Drago in such a rage on more than one occasion, and he knew it wasn't just bluster. The sheriff seldom made idle threats.

As he skittered off toward the saloon, Cloyd drew his Colt, cocked and eased back the hammer several times, and murmured to himself about what he'd do to the sheriff the next time Drago felt like threatening him. He was angry and scared all at once, and a growing panic welled in him over where the stolen loot was and if he'd ever see his share. His hatred for and mistrust of Drago had reached about as far as they could stretch. He must find that stash, and he knew he'd have to come up against the sheriff sooner or later. He had plans to make for when that time came, and he had to make them quickly. He passed the saloon and went directly to his room to straighten everything out in his mind, to find some answers to his present state of confusion. He knew he was to blame for the sad state of affairs, but he just couldn't get Flower out of his mind for days after every time he'd see her. She was the most beautiful woman he'd ever known, and his desire to someday have her for his own wife, as irrational as that was, burned in him with a flame nearly as hot as the blacksmith's forge.

"What was that weasel Cloyd doing here? Why would he be fool enough to walk right into my house when he knew I wasn't here? Answer me that, woman."

"I don't know. I was fixing to start some bread, and the door opened. I thought it was you coming home early, but there he was, bold as you please, grinnin' and smellin' like a dead skunk and acting like he was fixin' . . ."

"Fixin' to go kissin' on a real woman, I'll wager. If you wouldn't strut around town, showin' the whole world that fine figure of yours, men like him wouldn't pay you no mind. But, no, you have to tease 'em with your paradin' around all flouncy and such in that gingham stuff you keep orderin' from the Sears, Roebuck catalogue," Drago said, slowly working himself up into another fit of anger. "I never shoulda given you that thing."

"I have no idea where you got such an idea. I swear to you, I have never paraded around town even once. And I only wear my dress when I go to church—not that you'd know anything about that. As far as Cloyd is concerned, I view that man with nothing but loathing and disgust, and you know that. I've told you to get rid of him before he turns on you, and now what I said is coming true. Mark my words, you'd better watch your back around that man. He's got a devil in him," Flower said, hoping she had turned his thoughts away from giving her another beating and on to Cloyd, where they should be.

Drago stopped advancing toward Flower. He began

rubbing his chin in thought. What she had said made more sense than she realized. The money they'd stolen would surely be a high priority to the deputy, and the only thing that Drago had to keep himself from getting dry-gulched was that Cloyd had no idea where the money was. Or did he? Since his deputy was acting pretty bold lately, Drago suddenly began wondering if Cloyd had stumbled onto the hiding place of their ill-gotten loot.

Her husband's attention temporarily drawn away from her, Flower turned back to her kitchen duties, hoping and praying he'd not ask if she'd been in town before Cloyd showed up. She also choked back a fear that Cloyd, now spurned and embarrassed at being caught, might spill what he knew, or thought he knew, about Flower's buying a ticket on the next day's stagecoach. She hoped the trip would take her away from the constant threat of reprisal from her drunken husband.

As she took a step toward the counter, her foot brushed her cloth handbag, which she had dropped when startled by Cloyd's bursting in the front door. She glanced down in horror as she saw that the stage ticket had fallen out and lay next to the bag, in plain sight. In a panic, she tried to scoop up the handbag and ticket before Emmett noticed.

"What's your bag doin' on the floor?" Drago said with a frown.

Chapter Twelve

Kelly scanned the horizon for any signs of their riding into a trap as they broke camp the next morning. If
Spotted Dog had remembered the spot where he was
shot, the marshal hoped to find the answer to why someone shot him in the first place. It didn't make sense that
his own people would take him this far away from the
reservation just to dry-gulch him. Whatever the truth
was, Kelly aimed to find out. And soon.

"Which way are we headed, Spotted Dog?" Kelly
said as they mounted up. His black gelding snorted and
shook its head at the sound of its master's voice. Kelly
slipped his Winchester back into its scabbard and prepared to ride.

Spotted Dog pointed in the direction of a series of
hillocks off in the distance at the foot of another mountain. The purple hills beyond looked to be more than a

couple days' ride, but the rugged granite and wind-carved sandstone wilderness the Indian seemed to be heading for should only be about two hours more. That suited him just fine, because he was weary of the saddle and not a little impatient to get back to town. Back to Nettie's cooking. Or at least he was trying hard to fool himself into thinking it was her cooking he missed.

"I've got this strange feelin', Kelly," said Stevens after riding several miles across unfamiliar ground. "Somethin' just don't seem right."

"Yeah. I feel it too. Keep a sharp lookout for anything out of the ordinary." He eased the Winchester from its scabbard and rested it across the pommel of his saddle.

After another couple of hours, Spotted Dog said, "There, that is the place where we made our camp." He led the way down into a ravine with a dry creek bed running through it. Dotted all around were steep hills, giant boulders, and brush dry from the lack of rain for months. And above it all, buzzards circled lazily in the very direction Spotted Dog was leading them toward.

Prickly pear cactus was in abundance, chewed badly at the tips, evidence of the presence of the musky-smelling javelina, wild pigs with razor-sharp tusks.

Spotted Dog had disappeared into the brush ahead of the others when a cry came from where the Indian had gone. Kelly and Stevens spurred their mounts in pursuit down a narrow, sandy trail probably used mostly by mule deer and coyotes.

They pulled up short as the scouts scattered through

the rocks and brush. Spotted Dog was standing in the middle of a grisly scene, his arms pointed toward the sky as he chanted a pitiful, mournful song. On the ground around him were four corpses, clearly dead for several days. Their bodies had been torn at by whatever wildlife felt the need of a meal. As the buzzards circled, the grunts of several javelina running through the low brush made Kelly's skin crawl. The stench was unbearable. He and Stevens dismounted, walking their horses back up the trail several yards, upwind of the dead men. The scent of a dead human would often spook a horse.

"Are these your people, Spotted Dog?"

The Indian stopped his chanting and turned to Kelly with eyes ablaze. "The ones I came here with, the ones who shot me. But I wished them no harm—not this."

Kelly thought he might have seen the hint of tears in the old man's eyes.

"John Henry, we'd better get these bodies into the ground, and quick."

The sheriff was standing off to one side, about to gag at the sight. "I ain't never seen nothin' like this before, Marshal. Who would do this? It looks as if they were shot down as they were fixin' to eat, bunched around the fire, and all."

"That's how I see it too. They were ambushed. You got something to dig some holes with?"

Before Kelly could start scraping at the sandy soil with a fold-up shovel from his saddlebag, Spotted Dog snapped, "No! It is for my people to bury our dead, in our way."

Kelly nodded and backed away as the five Indians began their task of disposing of the bodies with an elaborate ceremony. Two began gathering dry brush and sticks, piling them into four separate mounds. They took blankets from their own horses and wrapped each corpse in one. Then they started four fires and placed the bound bodies in the middle of the funeral pyres. For over two hours the fires were kept blazing by adding more wood and brush until there was nothing left to burn.

When the fires finally died down, the Indians scattered the ashes about with sticks, eliminating any sign that lives had been lost at this place. Kelly began looking around for evidence of who might have murdered the four Indians. The bodies had been so badly decomposed, there was no way of determining even what caliber weapon inflicted the fatal wounds.

But it was clear by the way the men had fallen, they had been cut down in a fusillade of gunfire that left them no chance to defend themselves. Only one of their rifles appeared to have gotten off a shot; the other three were still loaded and left in the sand and gravel around the campfire right where their owners fell. The attack could not have been termed a battle, for only one side was engaged in the few seconds of firing that cut the four men down.

"These must have been the Indians Sheriff Drago claimed to have trailed from the robbery site and killed in a pitched battle. But the evidence shows something far different—not an exchange of bullets but a massacre," Kelly said angrily.

Sheriff Stevens grunted his agreement.

"And I'd sure like to know why they didn't even have the decency to bury the bodies," growled Kelly.

Kelly was determined to find out why the Liberty sheriff would have reason to claim something different than what the scene that lay before him would indicate. And if these Indians *had* robbed the stage and killed the guard and driver and passengers, what had they done with the strongbox and its contents? According to Stevens, Sheriff Drago had said he figured they had hidden it before he caught up to them. But surely there would be something lying around to indicate their having a connection to the stagecoach holdup.

"John Henry, I'm going to poke around the area for a bit, see what I can dig up."

"I'll just mosey on over to the others and keep an eye on things. Call out if you need me," said the sheriff as he left the shade of a cottonwood along the creek.

The five Indians were sitting on the ground, swaying back and forth, engaged in some sort of muttered chant— probably a way of showing respect for their dead, Kelly figured. He didn't want to interrupt, so he began scouring the area alone. Finding any indication of where someone could have hidden the stagecoach's strongbox was uppermost in his mind.

Several things had struck him as odd: The first was the absence of any evidence that these Indians were

anything other than what Spotted Dog said they were—
hunters. But even on that note, he couldn't understand
why they had come this far from the reservation for
meat, when they would have had to cross at least two
valleys, through which there was plentiful water and an
abundance of wildlife. And if they came so far, how did
they figure to get freshly killed game back across the
desert before it rotted? They were at least four or five
days' ride from the San Carlos. Maybe, he finally had
to concede, the old Indian just didn't yet trust him
enough to confide in him. Yet even that brought with it
a multitude of questions.

He found the going rough, climbing over large boulders that had broken off the face of sheer cliffs to come
crashing down in what must have been a dramatic event
centuries ago. *Glad I wasn't sitting in the shade of that
overhang when all that happened,* he mused.

As he got to the top of a rise where the narrow trail
petered out, he noticed a dark area where it appeared
blood had soaked into the dry ground. And a significant
amount of it, at that. He looked back in the direction of
the Indians' camp but couldn't see it. Changing position several times, he could find no clear view of the
place the four Apaches were cut down. He started back
down the winding trail to find Spotted Dog.

Cloyd cowered in his tiny room above the general
store and wished he'd never let himself do something
so foolish as to go to Drago's house and try to make
time with Flower. Whatever had gotten into his head,

anyway? If it had been someone else, he'd be the first to scratch his stubbly chin and say the fool must be tetched in the head.

He sat on the edge of his iron bed. Its rusty springs squeaked with every move he made. He held his Colt in his hands, turning it over and over, then half cocking it and spinning the cylinder, thinking he might have to use it before long to defend himself. He didn't like the idea of a confrontation with Drago, at least not one where he could end up lying facedown in the dirt with people standing over his body clucking their tongues and muttering about how stupid he'd been to come up against a known gunman like the sheriff. In fact, Drago's reputed prowess with a six-shooter was the very reason the town had asked him to run for sheriff in the first place.

These last few days hadn't gone very well at all for the scraggly deputy, and his future wasn't looking any too bright right now. If he could get his hands on the loot from the stage robbery, he'd pack up and head for Texas, maybe get on with a cattle drive going north. Anything to get him away from Liberty and a life that was looking bleaker by the minute. He had to come up with a plan for finding the money, something better than going down to the old abandoned mine with Devlin, acting as if he was searching for gold in order to get a better look around.

Just then he heard a knock at his door. He cocked his Colt as he walked across to place a hand on the knob. "Who is it?"

"It's me, Cloyd—Devlin. Let me in. I gotta talk to you. Hurry."

"Oh, all right. Hold your horses."

Cloyd gingerly opened the door, half expecting Drago to be behind Devlin with a shotgun, ready to blast them both to Perdition. But Devlin was alone. As soon as he slipped inside the dimly lit room, he shoved the door closed behind him. Devlin was out of breath, perspiring something awful, and stinking up the room with the smell of sulfur and rotten mud.

"What's so important you have to come stompin' in here, raisin' a ruckus?"

Devlin bent over and put his hands on his knees, out of breath.

"You ain't . . . goin' to believe what I found . . . down at the mine, Cloyd. Y-you ain't never, I tell you. You . . . thought I was just some crazy old coot that'd . . . never strike anythin' more important than water. But you was wrong, and . . . I aim to prove it to you. C'mon, we gotta get our horses and get back to the mine," Devlin sputtered, gasping for air.

"I thought I told you never to go back there without me," Cloyd said with a serious frown.

"Never mind that now. What I got to show . . . will make up for my not listenin' too good."

"All right, what'd you find, Devlin? C'mon, spit it out. I ain't got time for no guessin' games."

"Can't tell you—gotta show you," Devlin said. "Now, you comin' or not?"

A chill came over Cloyd as he suddenly realized that

Devlin might be talking about finding a stash of money. *His* money! And what would he do if that were the case? He slipped his Colt back into his holster and, with a furrowed brow, followed Devlin to the door.

Chapter Thirteen

Marshal Piedmont Kelly stepped out from the tangled brush alongside the meandering trail that led to the top of the ridge he'd just come down. He strode into the small clearing where Spotted Dog and the four Apache scouts were closely huddled in animated conversation. Sheriff Stevens had settled onto on a patch of dry grass nearby, slumped against a small granite outcropping with his hat pulled low over his eyes, snoozing.

The Indians were involved in an increasingly heated debate over something, speaking excitedly in their native tongue, little of which Kelly understood. He stepped between two of them.

"What is the problem here?"

"This is the dwelling place of evil spirits. My brothers say we must leave at once," said Spotted Dog.

"I understand why you must feel uncomfortable bein'

here where your people died, but we have to find out what happened before we can ride out," said Kelly. "You are gonna have to trust me. Nothin' will happen to you as long as Sheriff Stevens and I are with you."

One of the scouts still insisted they could no longer remain in this spot that was full of ghosts and death; soon the spirits would return and claim more of the Apaches. Two of the others mumbled their temporary acceptance of Kelly's assurances. None made a move toward the horses.

"Spotted Dog, I'd like you to come with me," said Kelly, trying to change the subject in hopes of dissuading the scouts from leaving just yet.

The old man moved quickly toward the marshal. His companions started to follow, but Kelly held up a hand. "Just Spotted Dog. We'll be back soon."

The looks on the faces of the four scouts indicated their mistrust of almost anything a white man did, but they complied after a reassuring nod from Spotted Dog and squatted back down, continuing to argue among themselves.

The old Indian followed in Kelly's footsteps as they wound around boulders and stumps of cholla and prickly pear cactus, the rocky ground crunching beneath their feet.

"Is this the way you came to get to the top of the ridge where you said you were shot?"

"Yes. I follow the track of the deer."

"Take me to the exact place you were shot."

Kelly fell in behind the surefooted Apache. After

several minutes they arrived at precisely the spot where Kelly had found blood splattered in several places on the rim of the overlook. The bloody trail gave every indication of a man's having been shot, then falling and rolling down a steep incline on the other side of the ridge. A bloody handprint on the surface of a jutting rock proved the victim had not been an animal. Spotted Dog was telling the truth about what had happened to him.

Kelly squatted down, looking for evidence of any other human tracks, and found a single set of boot prints. It occurred to him that he might have just discovered how Sheriff Drago came to be in possession of Spotted Dog's Spencer rifle. He stood up to determine if it was possible for someone around the campfire to have made such a shot and quickly realized that Spotted Dog's companions could not even have seen him, let alone shoot him, unless one of them had followed him up the trail. He doubted that could have happened without the wily old Indian's knowledge. He began scanning the terrain for the most likely position of the shooter. Off about fifty yards, atop another ridge with some good cover and nearly level with the place where he was standing, he spotted what appeared to be a good vantage point to get off a clean shot. As he squinted nearly into the sun, he saw something else that intrigued him: a dark opening in the rock face that looked very much like a cave.

He and the old Indian went back down to where Stevens and the others were now just milling around. Stevens had rolled a smoke and was about to strike a match on his britches when Kelly came into view.

"What'd you find up there on the rimrock?"

"I found plenty of evidence that Spotted Dog was tellin' the truth about where he got plugged. Blood all over the ground and rocks, just like he claimed. But there's somethin' else I'd like you to see. It's up there, across that little gulch, at the top of the knoll about fifty yards south," said Kelly, pointing to a boulder-laden hilltop.

Stevens squinted in the direction Kelly pointed, then nodded, stuffed the unlit smoke into his shirt pocket, and said, "Lead the way, Marshal. The sooner we get to the bottom of things here, the sooner I can get back to the comforts of home. I'm a mite eager to settle these old bones onto my own mattress instead of the hard ground."

"I could use some home cookin' myself," said Kelly.

"Don't you mean a little company from Miss Nettie? I saw the way you looked at that gal, and I could almost read what was goin' on in your head—not that it was all that difficult." Stevens snickered.

"Now, John Henry, you don't have any idea what was on my mind. I'm just gettin' a mite hungry for somethin' that doesn't almost yank a man's teeth out tryin' to chew it," Kelly insisted. "You might as well come along, Spotted Dog. If I'm right, you'll find this mighty interestin'."

"Uh-huh. Well, let's get a move on and climb that ridge," Stevens said as he struck out in the direction Kelly had indicated, eager to find something worth looking at. If Kelly was right, it would be about fifty yards east and up a steep incline.

When the three of them reached the foot of the ridge,

they found a trail that had recently been traversed by four horses, all shod, with one set of the tracks looking very familiar. Kelly bent down to get a closer look.

"Spotted Dog, that roan you been ridin' belonged to a man who was murdered in my camp while I was asleep. His horse left a distinctive mark in the dirt because its right rear shoe was broken. Look there. These are the same hoofprints. That man was on this trail not more'n ten days ago. Probably just before comin' into my campsite," said Kelly.

The Indian glanced up and down the trail left by the riders. He squinted as he looked toward the summit and the sun struck him square in the face.

"Four horses. Why they come here?"

"If I'm right, they had just come from robbin' a stagecoach. I think the man, George Alvord, whose horse made that track, was one of those robbers," said Kelly.

"Marshal, are you sayin' it was white men done the robbery, not them dead Indians down there?" said Stevens.

"That's what I'm thinkin'."

"So, it could be that Drago and his men tracked the wrong horses. Maybe they mistook the Indian ponies' tracks for the ones that done the killin'. That about what you got in mind?"

"That would be one possibility. Let's get to the top and see if there's anythin' to tie this bunch to the robbery."

They found the climbing difficult on foot, all three wondering what the four men had been thinking when they took their horses to the top. On the other hand, if someone didn't care all that much for his horse's legs, he'd probably be better off riding instead of getting himself all cut up on the barbs of the multitude of cacti that lined the narrow trail.

At the top, most of the vegetation had ceased to exist, unable to survive among the arid sandstone cliffs and dry, sandy soil constantly exposed to wind and blistering sun, and not enough water to quench a bug's thirst. But Kelly had little interest in what could or could not grow on the rough rock face or even survive in the harsh climate; he was drawn to the dark cave that had been carved out by winds and blowing sand over eons. The tracks of four horses led right to the entrance.

The marshal bent down and scanned the ground for evidence of what the men had been doing up there. He found seven spent rifle cartridges lying in the sandy soil. Directly below this nearly hidden cut-out was where Spotted Dog and his four companions found themselves trapped by at least four men with a clear line of sight both to their camp and to the lone Indian on top of the opposite ridge. The shooters couldn't have missed.

"Here's the place you were shot from, Spotted Dog— not from below, and not by your own people. Someone else shot you *and* all your companions, someone who didn't want you sniffin' around and discoverin' their secret hiding place."

The old Indian took in the words he'd heard, then broke into a solemn smile, encouraged by the revelation that he hadn't been forsaken by his own kind and disposed of like a worn-out blanket.

Stevens was several yards away, standing just inside the cave entrance, letting his eyes adjust to the dark, when he shouted, "Marshal, you'd best come see this!"

The sheriff was pointing to an open, steel-wrapped wooden box half buried in the sandy cave floor. The stagecoach strongbox had been blown open by a shotgun blast and emptied, then tossed aside, as it was the only thing to tie the robbers to the crime. Kelly figured Alvord was in possession of some of that stolen money when he stumbled into the marshal's encampment. Kelly grumbled at himself for not displaying more curiosity about the contents of Alvord's saddlebags when he shackled the man to the tree.

Kelly scooped up the empty cartridges and dropped them into one of his saddlebags. Two were longer than the others: .44-100s instead of the more common .44-40s. *Maybe these can help lead us to the shooter,* he thought.

"John Henry, let's get back to Cochise. I think we've seen enough here—at least enough to convince me that Spotted Dog had nothing to do with the stage holdup," said Kelly.

"Reckon I'd have to agree, but that still don't point the finger at anybody in particular. How do you figure on findin' them that done it?"

"Fair enough question. I don't know yet, but I think I'll continue to follow that horse of Alvord's back to where it came from: Liberty."

"Liberty? How do you know it came from there?"

"The liveryman in Cochise said he had seen Alvord

on that horse several times, and he knew he came from Liberty. He also said he had heard Alvord was a friend of Sheriff Drago."

"You ain't sayin' Drago had anythin' to do with this affair, are you? Why, folks over there'd be mighty upset if they got wind that you suspected their sheriff of a robbery."

"I'm not pointing the finger at anyone yet. But I figure some of the answers might be easier to find if I can locate who Alvord's friends were. Maybe Drago can help with that information."

"Well, you just watch yourself over there. That Drago is a tough one—nasty temper, and not a man to turn your back on neither. Leastways, while I hear he's been a fair to middlin' sheriff, I also know he's backed down a few folks at the point of a gun just 'cause he hadn't taken a likin' to 'em," said Stevens.

"I'll keep that in mind, Sheriff."

Chapter Fourteen

Cloyd sent Devlin to ride on ahead. He had to go to the livery and saddle his horse before he could ride out. After Devlin had ridden off, Cloyd started down the rickety stairs that clung tentatively to the side of the building. But as he was about to cross the street to the livery, he saw something that sent a chill up his spine. Sheriff Drago came out of his office, mounted his horse, and began slowly riding in the direction of the old mine, where Devlin had been spending his time hacking away with his pickax in a feverish attempt to strike it rich. Cloyd had come uncomfortably close to being in the saddle on his way out to the mine to find out what Devlin was so all-fired excited about when he saw Drago saddle up. He stepped back into the shadows to wait until the sheriff was out of sight. Devlin had had a good head start, so he probably wouldn't be seen.

Cloyd had never really had any intention of helping his friend look for gold. He saw the old man's search as a futile effort to discover something that wasn't there. If there had been sufficient evidence of a vein worth mining, the previous owners wouldn't have abandoned the place, Cloyd reasoned. And now he needed to stay clear of Drago, for fear the sheriff would revisit his being caught red-handed trying to smooth-talk Flower into something sinful.

But now, seeing Drago leave town, looking as if he was headed for the mine, Cloyd was curious, as well as concerned about Devlin's being discovered. He hurried around to the back of the livery stable, where he kept his horse in a small corral. He threw a blanket and saddle onto the mare, quickly mounted, and urged the animal to a slow walk in the same direction Drago had taken several minutes before. He intended to stay well back and out of sight; he could track Drago's horse easily by its tracks. He was convinced they would lead directly to the old mine, the place he had suspected was the hiding place of the loot from the stage holdup. If, indeed, that dark and forbidding old cave *was* Drago's intended destination, Cloyd saw this as an opportunity to confront the sheriff and take his half of the money—at gunpoint, if necessary. That would be more than enough to get him to someplace where he wasn't known and secure him the peace of mind afforded by such anonymity. The thought of getting his hands on all that money overshadowed any concern he might have for Devlin's being smack in the middle of it all.

As he approached the entrance to the mine, he reined in his horse behind a stand of mesquite and dismounted. Drago's tracks led straight to the entrance, just as he had thought they would. Cloyd eased out of the saddle, tied the reins to a low-hanging branch of a tree hidden from the entrance, and quietly made his way toward the dark opening. That's when panic set in. There, off to one side, grazing on some stubbly grass, was Devlin's horse. He'd almost completely forgotten the old man. He rushed to the entrance, where he heard angry words being exchanged between Drago and someone else. Cloyd's heart was beating a mile a minute as he slipped inside and began easing along the black tunnel, careful to let his eyes adjust to the darkness before getting too far inside. The voices became louder. He could finally make out for certain that the other person was Devlin. Drago had surprised the old gold hunter and was furious at finding him in the mine.

"Devlin! I asked you, what are you doin' in here?" Drago challenged the man.

"Lookin' for color, I told you. What's it to you?"

"What makes you think you can come in here and start digging for gold, you old fool? Don't you know this is private property? I oughta haul you down to the jail and lock you away until the judge gets here next month," Drago grumbled.

"This here mine don't belong to nobody no more. I checked the records at the county office. The ones what owned it gave up all claims when they walked away from it five years ago. You can't make me get out. I've as much right to be here as you do. So, what do you think of that, *Mister* Sheriff?"

Drago's hand fell to his six-shooter, and in a flash he was pointing it at Devlin's head, cocked and ready.

"This gives me some extra rights, Devlin, so your choice is to leave right now, or get blown to kingdom come."

"Folks know where I am, and they'll come lookin' for me. You don't want that, do you? And do you know why? It's because I found somethin', somethin' that shouldn't oughta be here," Devlin said with a confident snort.

"What would that be, old man?"

"That would be the loot from that stagecoach you said was hit by Indians. You said one of them got away with all the cash, but here it is, all packed up pretty as you please right there in a wall crevice. And you'll never guess whose saddlebags the money was stashed away in: yours. Don't take a genius to figure out it was you who robbed that stage and killed all them people."

"You think you got it all figured out? Well, let me tell you one more little fact you forgot: You may have found the money, but there ain't nobody goin' to hear a word of it, and do you know why that is, old man?"

"Nope. But I'd say that unless you cut me in on the money, the whole town is about to know what you done."

The blast from Drago's revolver echoed down the tunnel like a dynamite explosion. Dirt and debris fell from the ceiling and sides of the tunnel, and small rodents could be heard skittering among the clumps of rock and dirt, attempting to escape whatever terrible thing was happening. White smoke and the smell of cordite filled the closed space.

Devlin lay sprawled at Drago's feet, flat on his back in an inch of water. A hole in the center of his forehead left no doubt that the old man was dead.

"I reckon the town will have to wait awhile to get that information out of *you*," Drago sneered as he holstered his weapon and slipped through the narrow opening back to where he had stashed the loot from the holdup.

"No! Devlin, you sidewinder! Where did you hide my money?" Drago shouted into the darkness as he reached into the crevice, only to find it empty.

When he crawled back through the hole, he noticed that light from another lantern was illuminating the whole area where he had left Devlin's body, and as he looked up, he was staring right into Cloyd's revolver.

"What's the matter, Drago? Somebody playin' a little hide-and-seek with you?"

"Cloyd! What the devil are you doin' here?" Drago got to his feet and brushed the dirt from his pants. He then sat down on a large stack of wooden pilings that had been brought in years before to shore up the sides of the tunnel against cave-ins. He removed his hat and wiped his sweaty brow on his shirtsleeve.

"I was just ridin' by when I heard a shot. Thought I'd come and investigate. Ain't that what a deputy is supposed to do?"

"You was followin' me, and don't you try to deny it, you little weasel."

"Maybe, maybe not. Don't make a whole hill of beans,

does it, seein' as how you lost our money and there's a dead body lyin' at your feet."

Drago just shook his head and sighed. "Confounded, meddlin' old fool," he mumbled. "All that trouble and the money's gone. And all because of that old man's snoopin' around."

"Well, I wouldn't say it was gone forever, Sheriff. Might take a little huntin', but I'll bet it ain't as far from here as one might think."

"And how would you know a thing like that?"

"Time to make a deal, Drago. I need to be a full partner. No more you bein' in charge of the loot, and me bein' kept in the dark as to where it's hid. Fifty-fifty. You agree to that, we shake on it, and I'll set to findin' where the money's hid," said Cloyd. "We got a deal?"

Drago thought over the deputy's proposition for a minute. How could he refuse? If it got the money back, he'd probably make a deal with the devil—not that this wasn't about the same thing.

"Deal." Drago stuck out his hand, and they shook. "Okay, now where do we start lookin'?"

"I'd say you're probably sittin' on it," said Cloyd with a black-toothed grin.

"Wh-what? Sittin' on it? Why would you say a crazy thing like that?"

"Well, Devlin was out here diggin' for gold. I happened on his horse one day and found him in here. Whilst we was talkin', I noticed them beams was scattered all over the place. Now they're stacked up neat and tidy. I figure he hid the saddlebags under the timbers."

Drago didn't wait for any further explanation. Instead, he began yanking apart the pile of heavy timbers. Halfway down, there they were, two sets of saddlebags. He opened each one. All the money was there. Cloyd's instincts had been right.

"You're a lifesaver, Cloyd. I'd never have thought to look here."

"So, pardner, how about giving me my cut right here and now? Since you let Alvord and his cousin take half."

"Now, hold on. If that money starts showin' up around town, people are liable to figure out we had somethin' to do with the robbery. Best we keep it hid away until the right time," said Drago. "Alvord and his cousin promised to leave the Territory and not spend a penny until they were well clear of Cochise County."

"You're trying to pull another fast one on me, Sheriff. That ain't right."

"I said we'd be fifty-fifty partners, and I meant it. I'll stick to my end of the bargain—don't worry. But I don't want neither of us to end up stretchin' a rope. Besides, now that we both know where the money's hid, what could I do without your knowin' it?"

"I suppose that ain't a bad idea, but what do you figure on doin' with the loot?"

"Help me stack these beams back up. We'll leave them here for a while until we pull off another little plan I got," said Drago as he leaned over and began hefting the bulky timbers back into a pile.

"Plan? What kinda plan?" Cloyd decided to let Drago

do most of the work. Work was something Cloyd shied away from at every turn. He pretended to be trying to lift one log before Drago took it from him and heaved it onto the pile.

Winded from the exertion, Drago wiped at his face with a handkerchief he dragged from a back pocket.

"It's like this. This here money would last us, oh, say, about a couple years—maybe more if we was careful. But I figure what we need to do is build up our stash to where we can retire out in California for the rest of our lives. Providin', of course, we don't neither one of us do somethin' foolish, like gamblin' it away."

"How do we build up our stash?"

"We rob another stage, that's how. Then we put it all together, divide it up between us, and head out of this mangy town."

"You got a particular stage in mind, Drago?"

"I sure do. I hear that the coach comin' through to-morrow will be carryin' a lot of cash. We hit it about halfway to Cochise, just before they reach the stopover at Garcia's ranch. It'll be just the two of us this time. Split fifty-fifty."

Cloyd rubbed his chin as he thought over Drago's plan. He didn't really like the notion of robbing another stagecoach so close to Liberty, but the idea of making it the last one, then hitting the trail for California—really rich—sounded like a good plan.

"I'm in. That stage should make Garcia's about one-thirty or so. We could stop it at Devil's Pass before Garcia can even see it comin'."

"That's what I figured too. So let's head back to town and get ready for tomorrow. We'll leave early and be waitin' for them," said Drago.

"What do you figure to do with Miz Flower? She might not like being dragged outta her home to head off across them mountains," Cloyd said.

"Flower is goin' to have to figure out a way to take care of herself. She's done it before. I'm plannin' on leavin' without her. I've had my fill of married life, that woman always pryin' into my affairs."

As they mounted up and started back to town, the deputy was pondering an idea of his own. If Drago wanted to leave Flower, maybe Cloyd would, out of the goodness of his heart, just pick up the reins of that little filly and lead her to *his* watering trough. He would certainly be more understanding and tolerant of a female's needs. Why, he might even be convinced to take a bath once in a while, just as long as she didn't push that idea too hard.

He couldn't wipe the grin off his face at the thought of Flower and him getting hitched.

Chapter Fifteen

The Harken Brothers stagecoach that would carry Flower to Cochise was due in Liberty at around nine. Flower knew she would have a tough time explaining herself if she showed up in person at the stage line office and happened to be seen by anyone even remotely connected to her husband, so she figured she would meet the stage just outside of town. She could walk the half mile across country to a place on the dusty pike where she couldn't be seen from town but would still have sufficient shade to avoid heatstroke from exposure to the blistering rays of the midday Arizona sun if by chance the coach was delayed.

She'd gathered everything she owned of any lasting value and jammed it all into the large carpetbag, adding to the few things she'd put there earlier. She was now mad enough to make this trip to Cochise a permanent move. Although the bag was almost more than she could carry by herself, she figured to get an early start so she could rest along the way as needed. What she couldn't count on was where Emmett would be while she made her escape. If he got wind of her leaving, or if he caught sight of her himself, there'd be the devil to pay. And she'd be the one paying it.

Flower sat at the kitchen table, sipping the last of the morning coffee from a tin cup, trying to remember when she was last happy. *It certainly hasn't been during any of the time I've spent in this dirty little hamlet,* she thought. Mercy, how she'd grown to hate this town and nearly everybody in it, although she had to admit, she hadn't exactly gone out of her way to make friends. Emmett's jealousy was a major impediment to getting acquainted with many of the townsfolk, and certainly no men would be on his list of approved friends for her. And, frankly, she liked the company of men. She'd spent a good portion of her life singing or dancing for men in saloons or dance halls. Most men she understood, just not Emmett Drago.

The morning sun sent a shaft of light through the dusty window onto the floor, making a squiggly pattern. Emmett had risen early and left the house with little more than a mumbled, "S'long." She had no idea where he was headed, nor did she really care, except to be sure to avoid him when it came time for her to leave. And that time was rapidly approaching. Only a few more minutes remained for her to gather her nerve and strike out across the scorching sands to where she could hail the stagecoach for Cochise. She slipped a little .41 caliber Colt single-shot derringer into her skirt pocket just in case—in case of what, she didn't know. She only knew that nothing was going to stop her from leaving Emmett this time.

Twice before she had tried to strike out on her own, and twice before her husband got wind of it somehow and beat her to within an inch of her life. That wasn't going to happen again. That was the reason for the derringer, although she was loathe to admit even to herself that she could actually pull the trigger, sending another human being to the grave.

The town was waking up. Flower could hear the sounds of wagons being hitched to teams, men laughing and talking as they opened their stores for the day's trade, and dogs barking as if to be a part of the activity. The stage would be getting into Liberty in about a half hour. It would load any passengers and baggage for the next thirty minutes until its scheduled departure time. She planned to meet it just outside of town, on the western edge, as it reached that point an hour from now—about as long as it would take her to reach her intended place of boarding. There was no more room for vacillation. It was time to leave.

She lifted the heavy bag with a groan, wondering to herself if she really needed everything she had in there. *Too late now,* she thought. *I'm out of time for making changes.* So, with one quick look back, she hefted the bag out onto the porch and closed the door behind her. She let out a sigh as she started her trek northwest, behind the general store, across the empty lot where the Smiths' house had burned last year, and through a stand of trees that led down to the creek, now dry from weeks without rain. Perspiration began to trickle down her forehead as she struggled with the carpetbag, shifting it often from hand to hand, half carrying, half dragging it. An occasional groan escaped her lips from twisting an ankle on pebbles that were beginning to feel like boulders under her stumbling feet. Beaver tail prickly pear cactus barbs tugged at her skirts, and the odor of something dead nearby filled her nostrils. A breeze whirled dust around in tiny tornadoes, and she coughed as she inadvertently drew it into her lungs. This getaway was not proving to be a pleasant experience, and it crossed her mind to wonder whether living with Emmett was really worse than trudging across these burning desert sands. Then memories of being slapped nearly senseless by a man caught in the grip of demon whiskey brought her back to reality, and she found her resolve strengthened to keep going. Off in the distance she thought she heard the rumble of the stagecoach coming. She had better pick up the pace, or she'd be left standing there, with her only choices being to return to the hell she'd been living in, dragging that heavy bag back to a hot, drafty cabin, or to try walking to Cochise. Of course, that was out of the question. She would perish from the heat and lack of water before she got five miles. She somehow found the strength she needed, sucked in a deep breath, and lengthened her stride.

As the five Indians trailed behind in single file, Marshal Kelly and Sheriff Stevens rode side by side on their way back to Cochise. Few words were spoken between them for several miles, but that didn't mean there weren't plenty of thoughts swhirling around in their heads.

Stevens was the first to break the silence. "Just what do you suppose them Injuns was doin' camped out back there in the first place if they didn't rob that stage? Why wasn't they on the reservation, where they belong?"

Kelly didn't say anything for several minutes. He was lost in his own musings about the very same thing. He had come to be rather fond of the Spotted Dog, but he couldn't help thinking the whole truth hadn't yet come out. The old Indian was holding something back, and Kelly meant to know what it was.

"I think I know, but I'll wait to see if Spotted Dog tells me himself."

"Hmm. I reckon you know best. As for me, I'd as likely whip it out of them as palaver with a bunch of savages," Stevens said, letting his weariness from the long ride creep to the surface of his normally calm and reasonable demeanor.

"About the only thing I know is, I'd rather have folks volunteer information than me have to drag it out of them. Makes for a lot more trust, and trust is somethin' you need a lot of to stay alive in these parts," said Kelly.

"I reckon you know better than me about such things. But there's other things I don't understand about what's goin' on here. Take, for instance, the fact that them redskins was camped not a hundred feet from that strongbox. That's a mighty strong coincidence, don't you think?" Stevens said with a frown.

"Yes, it sure is. And it may all have something to do with the tracks we saw leading to the encampment."

"The tracks? What about them?"

"The Indian ponies were unshod, and their tracks were distinctive. Alvord's horse also left an easily followed trail, due to that broken shoe. Of course, we don't know who else was riding with him, but their prints were nearly wiped out by the ponies' tracks near the campsite. What does that tell you?"

"I can't say I follow you," said Stevens with a quizzical scowl.

"It says that the outlaws got there before the Indians," said Kelly. "And there weren't any later tracks."

Stevens frowned at what Kelly seemed to be implying.

As the little town of Cochise came into sight, Kelly reined in at the top of a small rise that led down into the shallow valley where the town had grown up around a gentle river that flowed for about three months of the year.

"Spotted Dog, you are coming with me. Tell the others they'll have to return to the reservation. Tell them you'll be safe with me," said Kelly.

The Indian did as he was told. The other four of his

people shook their heads, not wanting to leave one of their kind in the hands of a white man, especially not a lawman. But after a few minutes of palavering, the old man convinced them it would be okay, and the four Chiricahua scouts slowly rode off to the north in the direction of the San Carlos reservation.

Sheriff Stevens had ridden on ahead, unconcerned whether Kelly could convince the four Apaches to leave or not. He was only interested in getting some decent grub into his stomach and sleeping in his own bed instead of on the hard ground. As Kelly and Spotted Dog caught up to him, he turned to the marshal and nodded.

"I been thinkin' about what you said about those tracks, and I'm beginnin' to wonder just why Sheriff Drago thought it necessary to kill four young bucks without more evidence that they'd done the holdup," said Stevens. "And that ain't all I'm wonderin' about the sheriff."

"I intend to get answers when I get to Liberty. And that's where I'm headed, just as soon as I get this trail dust off me, get some decent grub, and get a good night's sleep," Kelly replied.

"We're startin' to think alike, Marshal. And I ain't sure that's healthy," laughed Stevens.

At a little past ten, the stagecoach rounded the bend at a good clip. When the driver saw Flower standing in the middle of the road, waving him down, he pulled back hard on the reins, bringing the heavy coach to a lumbering, sliding stop in a massive cloud of dust.

"What are you doin' out here all alone, miss? Don't you know they's Injuns and wild animals all around these parts?"

"Yes, driver, I am aware of all those dangers, but I am also aware of the dangers offered by drunks and gunslingers. That's what I aim to avoid by meeting you out here. I have my ticket," she said, waving the voucher in the air. "Now, may I get aboard?"

"Why, yes, ma'am."

The driver hopped off the seat, grabbed up her heavy bag, and secured it in the rear luggage boot. He looked briefly at the ticket she thrust toward him to examine as if he might not take her word for its authenticity, then nodded and opened the door to help her inside. She was the only passenger.

Climbing back into his seat next to the guard, he took the reins and whipped the horses to get up some speed before they started on the gradual grade that would take them over the hills and through Devil's Pass before they began the descent to their next stop at the relay station at Apache Bend.

"Did you ever set your eyes on such a lady, just wavin' purty as you please? I say, she's a looker, ain't she? If my missus could sense what I'm thinkin' right now, why, she'd never let me even step off the porch again," the driver said.

The guard riding shotgun grinned and spat a stream of tobacco juice onto the road.

Chapter Sixteen

The first place Kelly wanted to head for was the barbershop to get a bath and a shave before showing up at Miss Nettie's restaurant. Hungry as he was, he figured he could wait a tiny bit longer. He sure didn't want her to see him looking so shabby. Thoughts about her rambled through his mind like a mouse carefully picking its way through brambles. Something about her had made an unusually strong impression, something besides her obvious beauty. But he also had a feeling there was more to Nettie than she let on. The class with which she carried herself, her mannerisms—something suggested she might be more than just a grieving widow. He had every intention of getting to know her better.

As they turned onto the street the jail sat on, they saw that a crowd of about fifteen men, mostly made up of a rough-looking bunch of loafers and troublemakers, was gathering there. The deputy, Jed, was telling them to disperse and leave the law to its work.

"What's goin' on here?" shouted the sheriff as he dismounted and wrapped his horse's reins on the rail. "What're all of you doin' out here, makin' such a racket?"

"It's time you let us have that Injun before he gets away again and kills someone else." The faceless voice came from the middle of the pack.

"I want you to clear the street. Do it now!" Stevens insisted.

"We can't let folks get shot up by a bunch of heathens without them gettin' the justice they deserve," another one shouted, although without being brave enough to let himself be seen.

"This Injun didn't shoot anyone, and I can prove it. This here is a United States Marshal, and we both found evidence clearin' this man of any involvement with the stagecoach holdup and murders. Now, you folks let us do our job, and you go back to whatever you were doin' before you decided to cause trouble. Now, git!"

Stevens stood with his hand near his revolver, ready for trouble if it should start, but the group complied with his order and began dispersing, albeit not without plenty of grumbling and cursing. Most of the men headed for the nearest saloon.

"Try to get up a posse, and you get a couple of volunteers, but it don't seem difficult to raise a whole bunch of troublemakers to start a ruckus. It only seems to take a couple of drinks," Stevens mumbled as they climbed the steps to the jail.

"John Henry, I want to get cleaned up and get a decent meal into my belly. How about letting Spotted Dog stay here where no one can get to him until I'm ready to head for Liberty?" said Kelly.

"That'd be fine with me. Better he stays where I can keep an eye on him than have him wanderin' around where some drunken sidewinder might get an idea into his head to plug him."

"Spotted Dog, I'll bring you somethin' to eat after a bit," said Kelly. He then closed the door behind him and started across the street to the barbershop.

The old Indian said nothing but went to the first cell and laid back to rest. His wound was healing nicely, but he had been nearly overcome by a great weariness from the long ride back from where he and his people had been ambushed only a few days before. A little rest and some food would help sustain him for the ride to Liberty, whenever that came. The near certainty that he had been shot not by his own people but by some outlaws bolstered him. He had the marshal to thank for that. This man with a badge who read from a black book was clearly not like so many white men he'd known. Here was a man he could trust, he thought as his eyes fluttered closed from exhaustion.

As the stage rounded a blind bend at Devil's Pass, the driver was startled by two men wearing masks, sitting their horses right in the middle of the road. The driver had nowhere to go if he had any intention of trying to make a run for it. Boulders lined one side of the narrow roadway at that point, and a sheer drop-off lay on the other. The stage driver dug in his heels and pulled back hard on the reins, bringing the four-horse team to a shuddering halt. The guard brought his weapon up, intent on defending the coach, but before he could get a shot off, he was blown off the seat by a shot from a rifle held by one of the two masked men. He fell sideways off the stage and lay crumpled at the foot of a boulder, stabbed by dozens of spines of a prickly pear cactus.

Inside the coach, Flower was in a state of near panic. She dove for the floor, trying to squeeze her lithe body under the front overhanging seat. Her heart was beating like thunder, and she clamped a hand over her mouth to keep any involuntary sound from escaping to give her away. She could only pray that the robbers would leave her alone. She had nothing of value anyone would want, but then, she also knew that desperate men often looked at a woman in an irrational way. Silent tears began to flow down her flushed cheeks.

The stage stood still in the road, dust whirling around it as the masked men quickly dismounted and approached on foot, guns drawn and aimed at the driver.

"Toss down that strongbox, and make it quick," said one of the men.

The driver, recognizing he was in no position to argue, reached down between his legs, hauled up the strongbox, and dumped it over the side. He held up his hands, making it clear he intended to offer no threat to the highwaymen.

"You want me to look inside?" said Cloyd.

"Thought you said no one boarded back in Liberty. Ain't that what you said, Cloyd?"

"That's what I said, and I stick to it."

"Then why in tarnation do we need to look inside? I swear, if you weren't so good with a gun, I'd leave you out here to die of your own stupidity."

Flower instantly recognized the voices—Emmett and Cloyd! A gasp caught in her throat, and panic began to well up in her like a flash flood crashing through a canyon. She felt certain the whole world could hear her heart pounding in her chest, pounding so hard she feared it would burst. She scrambled to find the derringer she had put in her pocket, but it was caught under her, and she feared she couldn't free it without being heard. So she just stayed still, praying for a miracle, her eyes squeezed so tightly shut, she could see little multicolored stars dancing before her.

"Cloyd? Say, is that you, Sheriff Drago?" blurted the driver before giving sufficient thought to what such a revelation might mean to his well-being.

"Well, Harry, yeah, it's me. Sorry you figured that out."

"Don't you worry none, Drago. I got a terrible memory. Probably couldn't recall who it was by the time I get to Cochise. And that's for sure. Terrible memory. You j-just ask anyone," stammered the driver.

"I know you mean well, Harry, but the truth is, I just

Phil Dunlap

can't take that chance." And with that Drago cocked and fired his six-shooter twice, striking the driver with both bullets. Harry slumped forward and slid beneath the seat, dead.

"Cloyd, shoot that lock off and put the money into these saddlebags. And be quick about it."

Without a word, Cloyd did as he was told. One shot blew the padlock to smithereens, and within seconds he was scooping up gold coins and paper money, stuffing it all into the double bags Drago had tossed at him.

"That's it, Drago. I got it all. Pretty good haul, if you ask me."

"I didn't ask you. Now, let's get movin'."

With that, the two rode hard back toward Liberty, taking a circuitous route across the desert that would allow them to avoid meeting anybody who might be coming along the road. The stagecoach was left standing right where the robbery had occurred.

Flower stayed hidden for nearly half an hour before daring to stick her head up far enough to peek out the window to see if the killers had ridden off. Finally satisfied that she was, indeed, alone, she pushed open the door and stepped gingerly to the ground. She walked back to where the guard was lying facedown in the dirt. She didn't have to wonder if he was dead; she could tell by the way his body was crumpled up like a discarded overcoat and so soaked with blood that no one could have survived such an injury. She went back to the stage to check on the driver and found herself gripped with the same hopelessness as she hefted herself up onto the steel step rungs and peered over them, coming face-to-face with the open eyes of the driver, staring at her but seeing nothing. She let out a scream but knew it was for naught. It was merely an uncontrollable reaction to all she had seen and heard during the last hour and a half. She was suddenly gripped by a new fear—fear that she would die out there in the desert's building heat and not be found for days. She couldn't help but question her decision to run away from Emmett Drago, an act that had brought her to this point of near despair.

As he stepped onto the boardwalk that ran in front of Miss Nettie's restaurant, Kelly got a whiff of the collection of flowers planted in window boxes along the front of the building. A bee was busy drifting from one flower to another, collecting his daily meal. *Appropriate,* Kelly thought. *Nettie feeds the hungry both inside and outside.* As he entered, the aroma of bread baking caught his attention. He was so hungry, the slightest hint of real food was overwhelming. A bell tinkled as the door closed behind him. He took a seat at a table near the window, leaning his ever-present Winchester against the wall.

Nettie saw him and immediately came to his table. "Well, Marshal, it looks as if your last taste of my cooking didn't chase you away. I have some pretty good-looking steaks in the kitchen, just waiting for someone like you to order one," she said. "Potatoes, biscuits and gravy, beans, fresh bread . . . everything a hungry man could ask for."

Man alive, Kelly thought, *she is certainly a lovely woman. Why hasn't someone come and carried her away to a big, fancy house on a hill overlooking a lush green valley? Why is she struggling to keep a business going in this one-horse town?* But questions would have to wait. First there was the problem of satisfying an empty stomach.

"I'm hungry enough to eat it all, Nettie. And I reckon I'll take you up on that steak and beans. Sounds mighty fine. Hot coffee would be nice also."

"Coming right up," she said as she spun around and hurried off to the kitchen, disappearing through the curtained doorway.

When she returned a few minutes later, she was carrying some slices of fresh bread in a basket. She placed them in front of him with a warm smile. "Your meal will be ready in a few minutes."

"You know, I never even asked your last name."

"Cols . . . er, Colton. Nettie Colton."

"Say, I've been trying to recall the shooting in Tombstone that took your husband. I reckon I was up north when it happened," said Kelly.

"Oh, did I give the impression it happened there? Actually, it was up around Tucson. It was a few years back. I came down here to get away from the memory of that awful day," she said, nervously wringing her apron.

"My mistake, Miss Nettie. I probably didn't hear you

right. Besides, it's none of my business. Sorry to have brought it up."

"Oh, it's all right. I suppose it's just natural for a marshal to be curious about those kinds of things."

Chapter Seventeen

The marshal had just been served when he saw Sheriff John Henry Stevens coming across the street in a hurry, headed his way. Nettie was leaning on the back of an empty chair, watching Kelly with a smile of satisfaction as he took his first bite, when Stevens burst through the door, rattling the glass, and bringing with him a cloud of dust from a wagon passing by at that very moment.

"Your britches on fire, John Henry?" said Kelly.

"No, but the stage is overdue by nearly three hours. It just ain't like them boys to get off schedule by this much during the dry season."

"What are you figurin' to do about it?"

"I reckon I'd better raise a few willin' folks and go out and have a look-see."

"And you're also figurin' maybe I'd like to tag along, aren't you?"

"I thought you might be interested in makin' sure we don't have a repeat of what happened less than two weeks ago."

"You're right, but three hours overdue doesn't seem all that long, considerin' some of the stage drivers I've known," said Kelly as he leaned back in the chair, chewing.

"Maybe not for most, but these boys have been drivin' this route for quite a spell, and they don't make a habit of bein' late. I admit, I'm a little spooked by the last stage robbery and then seein' them dead Injuns and all. You got any suggestions?" said the sheriff.

"Well, if you can wait till I finish gettin' my belly full of somethin' more'n trail dust, I'll saddle up and join you. That suit you?"

"Suits me fine. I'll start roundin' up some others and meet you over at the jail."

"John Henry, I feel like something else might be botherin' you. Care to let me in on it?"

Stevens stopped halfway to the door, turned, and chewed on his lip for a moment. "You're right. A strange thought occurred to me. Now, I know the evidence has cleared those dead friends of Spotted Dog, but what if them four we sent back to the reservation decided to take a little revenge for the ones we buried out there, and this time, the Indians really *did* do it?"

"First of all, we don't know if anything has happened to get all het up about. The stage could have hit a rock and broken a wheel, or one of the horses could have come up lame and they had to round up a replacement at the relay station. Let's wait until we know something's wrong before we get too excited."

Stevens nodded as he left, grumbling about how some folks seemed to have all the answers, or something to that effect.

Nettie looked worried as she said, "Do you think there has been another robbery?"

"I hope not. The last thing this part of the country needs is a bunch of murderous outlaws chasin' the good folks away. No one wants to settle down when there's that kind of trouble. Speakin' of folks settlin' down, does this town have a church?"

"Indeed it does. Nice little church just up the hill. Why do you ask?"

"Just because I'm a marshal doesn't mean I'm a heathen. Thought I might visit if I'm around come Sunday, that's all."

"I-I didn't mean to imply—"

"Don't apologize. I know you didn't mean anything, but I guess I come upon a lot of folks who figure a lawman is no more than a gunslinger with a badge. Whenever I get a chance, I stop by a church. Kinda my way of rememberin' my father."

"I think I knew right off that there was something different about you, Marshal."

"Glad to hear it. And call me Piedmont."

"Perhaps I'll see you in church . . . Piedmont," she said with a hopeful smile.

He couldn't wipe the grin off his face as he polished off another piece of bread and took a swig of coffee before wiping his mouth with the cloth napkin and pushing his chair back.

"Ma'am, that was just about the best food I've had for months—come to think of it, maybe ever."

"My, how you do sweet-talk a lady, Mar—er, Piedmont. I'm obliged, however, to know I'm appreciated."

"Indeed you are, ma'am."

"Please call me Nettie. *Ma'am* sounds like I should be eighty years old. I'm not, in case you haven't noticed."

Kelly retrieved his Stetson from its peg, took up his Winchester, and started to leave.

"Oh, I've noticed, Nettie. Believe me, I've noticed." With that, he stepped from the restaurant and went straight to the livery where he'd left his horse for feed and water.

"Where we headed, Drago?" said Cloyd as the two spurred their horses toward a series of low hills off to the north. Once inside the tangle of cactus, mesquite, and paloverde growing like a jungle along a meandering dry creek, they slowed to a more reasonable trot to keep the horses from giving out from the heat.

"We're going to go back to Liberty the long way. I want to go up the creek for a while, then cut across that rocky promontory up there. That will throw off anyone figurin' to track us."

"Back to Liberty? Ain't that risky, us showin' our faces back in town right after a robbery takes place?" Cloyd was fidgety, and perspiration was pouring down his forehead. "What if people take it into their heads that we had something to do with it?"

"No one will think anything, you fool. We're the law, remember? Now quit fussin', and let's make tracks outta here," Drago growled as he broke into the lead.

They kept up an even pace for almost an hour before Drago pulled up in a draw surrounded by huge granite boulders. Their horses were heaving from the hard, hot ride, and Cloyd had started to complain . . . again. Drago figured it was best to stop and rest rather than have to listen to any more whining from his deputy. They let the horses drink from a burbling stream that flowed from a spring erupting from the side of a hill in the middle of a thick, green clump of cottonwoods.

"Where we gonna hide the loot, Drago?" Cloyd collapsed onto the ground in the shade of a tree.

"Same place we got the other hid. Who's gonna look there? We'll put it all together, sit tight for a day or two, then get on our way outta this county."

"You still thinkin' we oughta be makin' tracks for California?" said Cloyd, who had now leaned against the tree truck and was fanning himself with his hat.

"Or Texas. Or New Mexico. Maybe Santa Fe. They got some mighty purty gals up there in them cantinas."

"If it's gals you're lookin' for, how come you want to leave the purty one you already got?" Cloyd frowned.

"'Cause she's nosy and troublesome. I'm sick of her pryin' into my business. Besides, she's gettin' kinda wore out, gettin' a little age on her. I can see myself with a younger gal, someone with some spunk."

"I always thought Miz Flower was mighty special myself. Don't look like she's wore out to me."

"That what you were thinkin' when you went to my house? You *did* have somethin' on your mind other than a *friendly* visit, didn't you? I could see it in your eyes."

Cloyd became suddenly nervous, wiping his brow over and over with a handkerchief retrieved from his hip pocket. "Why, uh, no. And that's for certain. I-I just dropped by to, uh, say howdy. Just bein' neighborly and wantin' to be helpful. Didn't have no notion of nothin'— no, sir, not with Miz Flower. After all, she *is* your wife," Cloyd stammered.

"Not really. We was just pretend married. A bartender I knew up in Tombstone married us, although I might've led her to believe he was a travelin' judge. I don't rightly remember," Drago said with a devilish grin. "I never told her different."

Cloyd's interest in Flower grew with Drago's admission that he and Flower weren't really married. Maybe Cloyd's own dream could come true if he just told her the truth: that she was free to get married for real if she wanted. And he'd be more than willing to help her make that decision—in his favor, of course.

"Come on, Cloyd, we need to get back to town before they discover the stage. Then we'll be able to get a posse together and go after the low-down, lily-livered snakes that'd do such a thing." Drago roared with laughter at the thought. Cloyd even had to stifle a snicker as he envisioned the two of them leading a posse around in circles.

They mounted up and made tracks for Liberty and their mine-tunnel hideout. The coins in the saddlebags jingled as they moved over rocky ground, heading down into the valley. Drago was quiet as he began making plans in his head for how he would spend his money. And he certainly figured on all of it being his.

Sheriff Stevens had been able to interest only two others in coming along to check on the overdue stagecoach: the liveryman, Sam Arrowsmith, and the blacksmith. Kelly convinced Stevens that bringing Spotted Dog would be a good idea, since he was a natural tracker and would be able to cut a trail better than any of them. Besides, he figured that if it all turned out to be a wasted trip, he and the Indian would go on into Liberty and start their search for whoever had partnered up with George Alvord to rob and kill the other stagecoach driver, guard, and passengers.

At first Stevens was reluctant to bring the old Indian along, because he wasn't certain how the two townsfolk would take to riding with a savage, which most of them felt the Chiricahua were, but he relaxed after Kelly told him of his plan to continue on to Liberty afterward. Stevens liked the idea of having to keep an eye out for anything the Indian might try for only half of the trip.

But after his discovery at the Indian campsite where Spotted Dog had been shot and his friends murdered, Marshal Kelly was looking at the old Indian differently. While he was certain that Indians had not had anything to do with the holdup and killings, he also felt the old

Chiricahua was holding something back, not being entirely truthful about why he was out in the desert so far from the reservation in the first place. At least he wasn't ready to accept Spotted Dog's explanation at face value.

Kelly fell back and pulled alongside Spotted Dog. The Indian was staring straight ahead. He said nothing as Kelly approached.

"Spotted Dog, I'm puzzled by something. I can't seem to figure out why you and four of your people were at that campsite where you were shot. You said you were sent out to look for meat for your people, but you had to have crossed a number of streams where there would have been plenty of game. And you wouldn't have had to pack your kill so far to get it back. You weren't hunting, were you? You were running away from the reservation, probably headed for Mexico. Am I reading it right?"

Spotted Dog did not look at the marshal. He sat straight, never taking his dark eyes off the trail ahead. "You are right. I am sorry for the untruth. It has been a sorrow in my heart since you saved me from dying on that hill."

"Why did you run? Were conditions on the reservation that bad?"

"We were being cheated by men without liking for my people after the agent, John Clum, left the reservation. I had been a scout for the Army for many moons, and when I had no more value to them, I was sent back to the reservation to live among my people with nothing except my rifle and my clothes. No food, no money. Nothing. I ran, like so many others have done."

Kelly knew the reservations treated the Indians poorly much of the time. He hated the injustice, the poverty that he saw whenever he visited San Carlos, but he knew the strife between the Indian and the white man was a complicated issue, born of wanton killing on both sides. The basic mistrust of one for the other couldn't be resolved with simple answers. And so, he would try to gain the trust of this old Chiricahua, a man who had seen the Apache go from a proud nation to a scattered, desperate people preyed upon by everyone from common rabble and thieves to the government itself. He felt a strange kinship with this man, and he liked the way it felt.

"I reckon I can't blame you, my friend. I probably would have run too."

Chapter Eighteen

Flower was struggling to free her cumbersome bag from the luggage boot at the rear of the stagecoach. She was firmly in the grip of almost staggering fear. She was the only living witness to the wanton murder of two men—and the only one who could testify as to who the killers were. She shivered at the thought that she might have to sit in a courtroom and point to her own husband, condemning him to the end of a rope. Tears filled her eyes, trailing down her cheeks in salty rivulets. A hot, dry wind had picked up, making the dust it whipped into swirls cling to her skin; her hair was a tangle of curls broken free from the clasp with which she had pulled them back, tucking it all under her bonnet.

And now that bonnet was . . . where? What had happened to it?

She spun around to see if it had blown off as she

exited the coach. It wasn't on the ground beside the conveyance. She tugged open the door to see if it had been dislodged when she dropped to the floor to avoid detection by Emmett and Cloyd. It wasn't there, either. Had the breeze taken it from her head and blown it to who knows where? It was very light, made of straw, and could have fallen from her head without notice, especially under the circumstances surrounding the holdup. Her panic heightened as she envisioned Emmett and Cloyd coming back and finding her hat impaled on a nearby cactus, giving undeniable evidence of her having witnessed their crime. They would hunt her down no matter where she tried to run, of that she had no doubt. In that event, she would be as dead as the two men Emmett had just shot.

She rushed about trying to locate the little yellow chapeau, her favorite, the one without those dreadful, silly ribbons that tied around one's chin, one she'd brought with her from Tombstone. It was gone. And the time for her to try to escape this frightening place of death was nigh. She could only pray that her bonnet would never be found, at least not by Emmett Drago.

Finally she gave up the search, tugged her bag free, and let it drop to the ground with a dusty thump. She dragged it to the side of the road. What to do now? How could she ever hope to lug the bulky carpetbag and make it all the way to the relay station? Her head was awhirl in thoughts, spinning out of control, driven by almost debilitating fear. She must somehow gather her wits about her and make sensible decisions if she was to survive. Flower was no stranger to tough times, but she had never been in such a precarious predicament, one in which her life hung in the balance.

She shaded her eyes from the sun with one hand and dragged the bag behind her with the other. She reached down and pulled her skirts up between her legs and tucked the ends into her waist sash to make walking easier. Before leaving the coach, she looked for a canteen and found none. There might have been one in the boot under the driver's box, she thought, but the dead man's body was jammed so tightly into that space that she couldn't budge him. So, water or no water, Flower Drago struck out on her own across an inhospitable desert in the middle of a summer day.

After about an hour, she found herself getting dizzy, possibly nearing heatstroke from the lack of water. She looked around for someplace to sit in the shade and rest, to perhaps remain until later in the day when it might be cooler. But there was no shade, only bursage and needle-bristling cactus of every description. No streams, no trees, no boulders to tuck herself in under for respite. Just the unrelenting, blistering heat sucking the life out of her with each drop of perspiration that trickled down her forehead, dry before it could reach her cheeks. As she pulled the bag along, it snagged on a rock near the edge of the road, and she stumbled awkwardly with its weight, which seemed to increase with each hesitating step. The bag was finally wrenched from her grip after catching on a jagged rock, tumbling end over end into a ditch that ran alongside the road for a short distance. She barely noticed, too dazed from the heat and nearing exhaustion, so she continued on, dragging her feet now with every step.

After another hour, her strength finally gave out, and she collapsed at the side of the road, muttering to herself something about a lake of cool, fresh water only a few steps farther. She lost consciousness within seconds.

Late that afternoon, Sheriff Stevens, Marshal Kelly, Spotted Dog, and the two other members of the posse reined in at the top of a rocky promontory where they could overlook the valley through which the stagecoach should have passed. Kelly pulled the field glass from his saddlebag and began scanning the horizon to see if he could spot any reason the stage had yet to arrive in Cochise.

"You see anything through that there spyglass, Marshal?" said Stevens.

"No coach. The only thing I see is a colorful pile of something near the road. Looks like some fancy clothing fell off someone's wagon and landed in a heap. We'd better go down and take a look at whatever it is. Spotted Dog, you lead the way and look for signs of any recent tracks."

The Indian dug his heels into his horse's flanks and trotted out in front of the posse, deftly guiding the mare around clumps of cholla cactus. His dark gaze darted about like that of a hungry coyote on the lookout for prey. After about half an hour, they approached the still form of Flower Drago lying in the road, right where she had fallen hours earlier. The Indian was about forty yards ahead of the others when he realized it was not merely a pile of clothing, but a woman, lying very still. He signaled to the others.

"It is Anglo squaw!" he shouted as he galloped to where she lay and jumped from the horse. He knelt down beside her limp body and started to lift her to a sitting position.

Kelly was there in seconds. He, too, leaped from his saddle and rushed to where the woman had lain sprawled in the dirt, face up to the blazing sun.

Her face was blistered, and her lips were cracked and bleeding. She made a feeble groaning sound as the two of them held her.

"Get my canteen off my horse, Spotted Dog. She needs water badly."

The Indian returned with the canteen, twisted off the cap, and held the cloth-covered tin to her lips. She choked at their first attempts to get her to drink but finally got a couple of swallows down her throat.

As Stevens and the others rode up, Kelly turned to the sheriff and said, "Do you know who this woman is, John Henry?"

Stevens dismounted to get a better look at her. "I've never laid eyes on her. She looks to be in bad shape, though. What in tarnation would possess a woman like that to be wandering around in the desert in the middle of the day? You suppose she's from a nearby ranch?"

"We've got to get her some help, and fast. She's sun-blistered bad, and she could die if we don't find a doctor," said Kelly. "Spotted Dog and I will go on and try to locate the stagecoach. John Henry, you three take her back to Cochise and get her some help."

"The relay station isn't far from here. We can at least get her inside, maybe borrow a buggy to take her to Cochise," said Stevens. He motioned for the other two to help get her onto his horse behind him.

The blacksmith took a length of rope and wrapped it around the girl and the sheriff to keep her from falling off as they rode. They started off across country toward the halfway point between Liberty and Cochise, where a small grouping of buildings served as a place to get food, water, and a short rest for the stage passengers while the horses were unhitched and fresh horses brought up to continue the trip.

Kelly and the Indian began backtracking the route the woman had obviously taken. Her stumbling footprints were readily traceable. They had traveled almost an hour when the stagecoach came into view. The marshal spurred his horse to a run as he saw the team standing still, switching their tails from side to side to chase away flies. As he came upon the coach and hopped down to get a closer look at what had happened to cause it to be stopped in the middle of the road, he could tell by the eerie silence that seemed to cling like the smell of a skunk to the scene, he wasn't going to like what he was about to find.

The buzzing of insects around the driver's seat led him to the first body. Spotted Dog found the dead shotgun guard several feet behind where the coach now sat.

Kelly pulled the driver's body down and dragged it to one side. The Indian waved him over to where the guard lay. The two of them lifted his body and carried it to the driver's. Kelly removed his hat and wiped his forehead with his handkerchief.

"Spotted Dog, see if you can find any tracks of the sidewinders who did this."

The Indian began the search and was quickly rewarded with plenty of tracks coming from the desert to where they found the coach. Kelly had begun examining the coach for any signs of who might have perpetrated this foul deed. He frowned as he opened the door. There, on the floor, lay a woman's silver hair clasp, wedged into a crack. He pulled it free and stuck it into his vest pocket. He saw where someone had pulled a bag from the rear storage shelf. A woman's footprints were all around the coach, the same footprints they had just been following. Spotted Dog came running up with a yellow bonnet in his grasp.

"Tracks of two horses. I find this on the spines of cactus." He handed the bonnet to the marshal.

"The lady we found on the road must have lost it. That's why she wore nothing to shade her from the sun. She was most certainly a passenger on the stage, but the men who killed the driver and guard didn't bother with her. Why? The driver's gun was still in his holster. If they killed him to keep him from exposing them, why leave her alive?"

"Tracks come from road but go toward mountain, there," said the Indian. He pointed in the general direction of where Drago and Cloyd had ridden to make their getaway, intending to throw off any posse set on tracking them down.

Kelly nodded his understanding and stood pensively for several minutes, considering whether to drive the stage on into Cochise himself or follow the trail of the killers. Finally he made a decision.

"Spotted Dog, tie our horses to the back. We'll put the bodies of the driver and the guard inside. Then you climb up on top with me. We're takin' the stagecoach back to Liberty."

Chapter Nineteen

Drago and Cloyd had ridden many miles out of their way returning to Liberty, keeping to the roughest terrain they could find. They figured sooner or later there'd be a posse out looking for them if they didn't get back home before the discovery, so they did everything possible to confound anyone who might track them back to Liberty. They followed dry riverbeds and cactus-choked gulches, rode over and around rocky projections and slickrock hillocks to escape detection. As the sun blazed on, they kept up a steady pace, pushing hard to return to town before the robbery was discovered, thus diverting any possible suspicion from themselves.

"We goin' straight to the jail? Or should we go to the mine first, Drago?"

Drago shook his head. "We can't go ridin' into town

155

with our saddlebags full of money, you fool. What if someone got curious and decided to take a peek before we got it all stashed away?"

"Oh, yeah, I see what you mean. You want me to take it to the mine alone? That way you could go on into town and see what's brewin'. You'd be there to get any news," said Cloyd.

Drago looked at him as if he'd lost his mind. "Sure, Cloyd, you take charge of the loot. I surely do trust you alone with all this cash. Why, I wouldn't even give a moment's thought to you maybe hightailin' it outta here faster than a jackrabbit with a coyote hot on its trail."

Cloyd pulled a face. "That's no way to treat your partner. Why, I wouldn't no more pull out on you than Flower would. We're partners, and I have a deep respect for that. You should too," Cloyd said with a pout.

Drago snorted derisively.

Just then, Cloyd had a flashback of when he'd seen Flower buying a ticket for the stagecoach. He wondered if maybe she *had* been thinking of running out on Drago. If so, he couldn't blame her. He'd seen the aftermath of Drago's hot temper too many times—bruises, black eyes, cuts. He'd often wondered why she stayed with him at all. Wouldn't it be fun to see old Drago's face if she did skip town? She probably would have done it long before if the old tightwad had allowed her to have a horse of her own.

He must have been grinning too broadly just then, because Drago looked over and growled, "What the hell you got that possum-eatin' grin on your ugly face for?"

"Who, me? Why, no reason, Sheriff. Just thinkin' about all the things this money'll buy when we light out for parts unknown."

"Well, wipe that grin off your face before someone starts askin' too many questions, and you end up blurtin' out the wrong answers like you usually do."

"Uh, yes, sir. I'll do that. I will," said Cloyd, but inside he couldn't stop having thoughts about him and Flower meeting up in some far-off romantic place and then ending up getting married. She'd have a real marriage this time, he mused. Like she deserved. And plenty of money.

Flower was slowly regaining consciousness when Elizabeth Garcia, the wife of the stationmaster who provided fresh stock for the stagecoach company, came back into the tiny bedroom to check on her patient. Flower groaned as she tried to sit up, then fell back with a gasp of pain. Her skin was bright red and had started to blister in places from her long exposure to the direct rays of the sun. Elizabeth kept putting cold, wet compresses on her face. Earlier, she had also brought in a tin can full of liniment to slather on the worst of the burns.

"Now, just you lay back there, sweetie. Don't try to get up. You're burnt pretty badly, and you need your rest. I brought you some broth to help you get your strength back."

Flower just looked at her through puffy, red eyes, not quite sure what to make of her situation. She tried to speak but got little more than a squeak out before the lady started to raise her shoulders and stuff some pillows behind her so she could eat. Getting her strength back was the farthest thing from Flower's mind at that moment. Fear of Emmett's finding her far outweighed any consideration she might have for food or much of anything else.

Elizabeth dragged a chair over to Flower's bedside and sat down. She raised a spoonful of chicken broth to Flower's mouth but soon found that the woman was too weak even to draw in a sip.

"You need to try to eat a little. That's the only way to get you well."

Flower just groaned and tried to shake her head. But as her skin touched the sheets, she took a deep breath to calm the scream that was rising in her throat.

"What's your name, honey?" asked the matronly lady, realizing that her attempts to get Flower to eat were wasted. Maybe she could at least get some idea of who this lady was and where she belonged.

Flower tried to speak, but the pain of her cracked and blistered lips was too great. All she could do was murmur incoherently.

"I understand. You get some sleep. Maybe you'll be able to talk in the morning."

That thought shot through Flower like bullet. *In the morning? Where am I? Am I safe from being found by Emmett?* Questions whirled inside her head like bees circling a hive; her stomach was in a knot at the prospect of being discovered by a man she had no doubt would rather shoot her than let her leave him. The lady who had tried to give her food left the small room.

Flower wanted to cry out for help in getting as far away from Liberty as possible. California, maybe, or at the very least, Tucson. No words emerged from her cracked, puffy lips. Her throat was as dry as the desert itself, and now she wished the lady had stayed longer and tried harder to get something down her. She drifted off to a restless sleep, destined to relive, over and over, in her dreams, the nightmare of the stagecoach holdup.

Elizabeth Garcia looked up as her husband entered the kitchen of their small home, a low adobe structure with a large eating area meant to accommodate hungry passengers when the stagecoach stopped for a change of horses. The kitchen that opened into a dining room was small but cheery, thanks to the homey touches added to barren walls by a woman who missed the old homestead in Fort Worth.

"Antonio, I can't get any food down the poor thing. I reckon her burns are too painful and her throat too parched to even swallow. I can't for the life of me imagine what could have possessed a woman like that to wander around in that dreadful desert."

Antonio Garcia filled a cup with coffee and sat down at one of the two long tables meant to seat eight to ten people each, just in case there were two stagecoaches in at the same time.

He had removed his hat when he came inside, hanging it on a peg next to the door. Elizabeth had scolded him often that she absolutely could not abide a man who wore his hat indoors.

"I can't either. And I'm worried about that stage too. Somethin' terrible has happened again. I just know it."

"Where'd that Sheriff Stevens and his men get to?"

"Sent the others back to Cochise, and then he rode on up the road to see if he could find the stage. I hope he don't find it like that sheriff from Liberty did the last one."

Drago and Cloyd approached the old mine late in the day but stayed hidden for a time behind some house-size boulders as they sat checking to make sure no one had stumbled onto the body of Devlin. They could scarcely risk being seen unloading their ill-gotten gains and secreting them away right beside a recently deceased corpse in a shallow grave. After several minutes of scanning the area to feel certain they were alone and hadn't been followed, Drago led off, motioning Cloyd to keep dead quiet as they neared the entrance.

Inside, where they could secure their horses from being seen by anyone riding nearby, Drago dismounted, pulling his saddlebags off with him. Cloyd did the same, and they started back into the dark tunnel after Drago touched a match to the wick of a lantern.

"It don't look like anybody's been here recently, other than us, of course," whispered Cloyd.

"How can you tell we been here?" Drago said as he glowered over his shoulder at the deputy.

"By them prints you leave. They're real easy to recognize. See? There's where you came out last time."

Drago looked down. *Consarnit! He's right,* he thought. *Any lawman worth his salt could tie me to this place. I gotta make sure I cover them tracks up good when we leave.*

"Cloyd, you go out and cut a couple branches off one of them trees. We'll sweep the place good as we pull out. Then there won't be no tracks to identify. I'll go back and stash the loot while you're doin' that," said Drago.

Cloyd didn't like the idea of leaving the sheriff alone with all that money. Heaven only knew what devilish plot Drago had drummed up for cheating Cloyd out of his fair share. But the deputy just nodded and started back the way they came in. He stopped, though, before getting to the entrance, turned, and retraced his steps. His plan was to sneak back down the tunnel and watch where Drago ended up hiding the money, so he could slip back later and get it himself.

If somebody's gonna get cheated, it ain't gonna be me, Cloyd thought. *I don't plan to let that money out of my sight again.* He kept close to the damp walls as he edged along in the dark, trying to avoid making any sound. He knew that if Drago caught him sneaking back into the tunnel without those branches, there'd be hell to pay. The sheriff was as mean as a snake, quick to kill and without remorse when it came to dispatching anyone who dared disobey his orders. But right now Cloyd was driven more by the fear of being cheated out of the money he'd killed for, risking getting caught and hanged for, than he was of Drago. So he continued slowly making his way, taking step after step with the care of a barefoot man on broken glass.

As he neared a bend in the tunnel, he could make out a dim light well past the pile of timbers where the two of them had replaced the loot from the first stage holdup. It was too dark to make out whether the money had been moved, but he could see Drago's shadowy form stuffing a handful of something into a wall crevice.

That snake is taking out some of our money to cheat me out of my full share, Cloyd thought. *Well, I'll just show him.* The deputy turned to go back outside to retrieve the branches he'd been sent for in the first place. But in his haste, and with not an insignificant amount of anger welling up in him, he failed to keep close enough to the wall, inadvertently twisting his ankle on a rock and splashing into a puddle of standing water.

Drago heard the splash and sent a bullet toward the sound. Cloyd made a hasty retreat. When the deputy got outside, he quickly cut a limb off a nearby cottonwood tree and then returned to the tunnel, shouting as he went.

"What is it, Drago? What are you shootin' at?"

Drago emerged from the dark to see Cloyd coming toward him. He blinked to let his eyes adjust to the brighter light.

"Was you inside, you little snake?"

"Me? Why, no. I been cuttin' limbs, just like you said to," answered Cloyd, a wide-eyed look of innocence pasted onto his face.

Drago just growled. "Musta been a rat or something. Bring them limbs inside, and let's get to brushin' out our tracks."

Cloyd hastily followed Drago back inside the mine-shaft. Fortunately for him, Drago hadn't noticed the deputy's sopping-wet pant legs.

Chapter Twenty

As Kelly and Spotted Dog neared the little town of Liberty, they could see groups of two and three riders from surrounding ranches or mines arriving in hopes of spending an evening drinking and gambling. The sun wouldn't set for another couple of hours, but already the hitching rails were filled with the reins of horses shifting from one foot to another, tails switching from side to side, keeping the blackflies at bay. Kelly drove the stage down the middle of the street, and people stopped to stare at the tall man slapping the reins and at the old Indian they'd just as soon wasn't hanging around town sitting atop the coach.

"Hey, mister, where's Harry and Ben?" said one of the men who approached as Kelly brought the coach to a dusty stop.

"Who are Harry and Ben?" said Kelly.

"The driver and the shotgun guard."

"They're inside, both dead. We found the stagecoach abandoned on the road, robbed of whatever was in the strongbox," said Kelly. He reached down into the boot and tugged the empty strongbox free, then tossed it over the side. It crashed onto the dirt street for all to see.

On their way into town, Kelly had decided not to let anyone know that he was a marshal. He had removed his badge and tucked it into his shirt pocket. He told Spotted Dog to say nothing other than that they were just drifters looking for a place to stay when they came upon the grisly robbery scene.

"You got any law in this town?" said Kelly.

"I'll go get the sheriff," said another man, already at a lope toward the clapboard-sided jail building.

"Good idea," said Kelly as he scrambled down from the driver's seat. Spotted Dog followed, then went to the rear of the coach to untie their horses and lead them to a nearby watering trough. The Indian also chose that time to splash water onto his own face, to wash off the dust that stuck to all stagecoach riders like molasses.

Seconds later, the man came back shouting, "The sheriff's not there! Deputy, neither! Anybody seen 'em today?"

Quite a crowd had gathered, but no one could recall seeing either Drago or Cloyd that day.

A man who identified himself as the undertaker rushed up and eyed the two corpses. "Looks like I got me some business to attend to. How about a couple of you fellas help me carry them to my parlor?"

The stage line office was at the far end of the street. Kelly told one of those milling around to drive the coach on to the office. He said if the sheriff got back, he'd be at the restaurant across the street, and with that, he and Spotted Dog left the murmuring crowd and went into the Liberty Diner.

When they entered, it was clear that the old Indian wasn't welcome. A heavyset, balding man came over to them as they pulled out some chairs to sit at a table near the front window, clearing his throat and frowning.

"Uh, sorry, gents, but I'm afraid we're all outta vittles. The cook took off, and, uh, I can't say when we'll be back in business." He turned his back on them before they could launch a protest, and he disappeared through a curtained doorway.

Incensed by the rude treatment, Kelly turned to fix his gaze across the room at two men who were just finishing a large helping of beans and cornbread. His first inclination was to follow the man who'd turned him away, stick a gun into his face, and let him reconsider the availability of some grub. But, though his temper had risen rapidly, so, fortunately, did his grip on common sense. He eased out of the chair, motioned Spotted Dog to follow, and sauntered toward the door.

"I'll go over to the general store and get us some hardtack and jerky. Looks like this town ain't none too friendly to strangers," said Kelly as he let the door slam behind him in a final act of defiance.

"Indians, either," said Spotted Dog as he grinned broadly to let the marshal know he understood.

Sheriff John Henry Stevens came to the place where the stagecoach had been stopped. He slipped from his saddle to check more closely the signs of what had occurred. Bloodstains on the ground at one side of the road told some of the story, but he could make out only that the stage had been sitting there for some time, with the horses shuffling their hooves and occasionally relieving themselves. It was clear that someone had been badly wounded or killed and the coach likely robbed. Marshal Kelly and Spotted Dog had ridden in, then appeared to follow as the coach was turned around and driven back the way it had come—by whom, he couldn't say.

Stevens stood in the roadway, chewing on his lower lip, convinced that outlaws had once again struck in his county. Fifteen years older than Kelly, he had seen the best and the worst the frontier had to offer. And there never seemed to be an end to the worst, an element he could only hope might be obliterated someday.

I wonder why Kelly didn't just take the stage on to the relay station, thought Stevens. He pondered this question for a moment, then turned to look for evidence of who might have stopped the coach. The tracks of two riders who had come from behind a rocky outcropping were clear to begin with, but he knew they wouldn't be for long, what with night coming on in only a few hours and the wind starting to come up, announcing the onset of a dry storm.

Stevens decided to follow those tracks for as long as he could, then make camp for the night. Maybe he'd get lucky the next morning. The one thing that bothered him the most was the way the tracks seemed to lead in no particular direction, just wandering around, following the most difficult terrain available. The outlaws didn't seem to be in any hurry to put distance between themselves and a posse. That struck him as strange, certainly not the behavior of most of the outlaws he'd known for the past twenty-odd years of being a lawman. He rode on, stopping often to dismount, looking closely for even the slightest clue as to where they might be headed. If these guys had robbed the stage, they knew what they were doing, he thought as he kicked a clump of dirt out of sheer anger.

"I got the wagon hitched up, and I'm ready to take the lady into Cochise," said Garcia.

His wife came to the door and waved him inside. "She's so weak, it'll take both of us to lift her into the wagon," Elizabeth said.

"I put down a good bed of straw so she don't get jostled too much. Best we wrap her up good so she don't get no more sun," he said. "Did you get some of that ointment onto her?"

"Much as I could. She cried out every time I touched her. Poor thing must be suffering something awful. I'd say there's a man behind this whole mess; cain't be no other reason for such foolish behavior." Elizabeth's voice cracked as the anger welled up in her from watching Flower in such agony and knowing there wasn't much she could do to help. It pained her to watch the woman struggle, not only with the discomfort of the burns, but something else that seemed to torment her, something deep within her.

Flower groaned as she was gently loaded onto the flatbed wagon. Garcia climbed into the seat and turned to his wife. "Are you going to be okay here by yourself? Might be a stagecoach come through at early light."

"I'll be fine. I've done changed horses more'n once when I had to. Don't think one more time'll kill me. Mercy, you're like an old hen worryin' about her chick. Now, go on with you, and mind you take it easy with your cargo. It ain't like you're haulin' feed," Elizabeth scolded with a mock frown.

Garcia waved over his shoulder and whipped the horses to a walk. The trip into Cochise would take several hours, especially since he had to drive so slowly. What Elizabeth had said about there being a man at the root of the woman's troubles rolled around in his head. He didn't like the idea that some men did seem to treat their women poorly, and he also didn't like the innuendo that lumped all men into that category. His marriage had been one of sharing equally the duties and responsibilities of managing the way station, something the two of them had done since they were first married in a small church in Tucson some ten years earlier. His only regret was that they hadn't had any children.

As he drove the wagon slowly, being careful to avoid the many holes in the badly rutted road and places where sudden, rushing waters had nearly washed the surface away entirely, he looked up to see a sight that sent a shiver down his back. Off in the distance, on the top of a hill several hundred yards away, he could clearly make out the silhouettes of four men taking in the scene below. They were unmistakable in the way they sat their ponies. Chiricahua.

"We got the footprints all swept away. Let's mount up and head for town before someone comes lookin' for us," said Drago.

"You figure they found the stage yet?"

"Hard to say. But we gotta be in town when they bring in the news."

Drago and Cloyd pushed their horses hard to make up for the time it had taken to get rid of the tracks that could lead someone to where they had hidden their stolen cash. Figuring it was likely that a posse would be mounted by the sheriff of Cochise, since the robbery took place closer to there than to Liberty, Drago was counting on Stevens' lack of familiarity with the area to help throw him off their trail. Wiping out their tracks to and from the old mine shaft had been a good idea, one he grudgingly had to credit to Cloyd.

Feeling confident that they had, once again, pulled off a successful holdup, the two of them slowed their mounts as they reached the town limits, to appear as if they had merely been out for a ride. But that plan was about to change, as Cloyd first noticed the stagecoach pulled up in front of the express office.

"Drago, look! The stage is already here. What do we do now?"

"Shush! You fool, someone will hear you. Calm down, and let me handle things."

They both dismounted and went immediately into the office, where the stationmaster was pacing back and forth, wringing his hands. Several other men were gathered around; all wore expressions of grief and anger.

"It's about time you got here, Sheriff. Someone robbed the stage and killed Harry and Ben," said one of the men.

"Yeah," said another, "you shoulda been here instead of out gallivantin' around. What do you plan to do about this?"

"Harry wouldn't have hurt a fly, and you know it. Weren't no reason for nobody to go shootin' him. He has a family—wife and kids. Who's goin' to take care of them?" shouted yet another.

"Now, hold on, all of you. I'll get to the bottom of this, don't you worry. Who brought the stage in?"

"Coupla strangers. A tall, lanky one and an Indian," said the stationmaster.

"Where are they right now?"

"Said they was goin' to the restaurant."

"I'll just go have a talk with those fellas, then," said Drago.

As Cloyd and Drago started down the street to find Kelly and the Apache, Drago said, "Indian, huh? I'm thinkin' we just might have ourselves a solution to this awful crime." The sheriff grinned widely as he hurried his steps. Cloyd followed right on his heels, slow to catch on to Drago's meaning but eager to be there when the confrontation occurred.

Chapter Twenty-one

S heriff John Henry Stevens had spent too many hours in the saddle, and he was growing weary from getting off his horse every few yards to reaffirm that he hadn't lost the trail of whoever had stopped the stagecoach, probably robbed it, and took off for the hinterlands to escape detection. It was tiring work, and he wished now he hadn't sent the other two men back to Cochise. The tracks were tough to follow under the best of conditions, and those conditions were worsening by the minute. Some sort of dry storm seemed to be brewing. Winds—hot, whipping, gusty winds—swirled about him. Sand, blowing up like ocean waves, bit at his skin and filled his eyes and nostrils. He pulled his kerchief up to cover his mouth and nose and pushed on, determined not to let the foul weather aid the outlaws in their attempt to beat the law.

After several hours, he had to admit he was lost. He didn't know this part of the Territory well. He spent nearly all of his time in town, and now he cursed himself for venturing out alone, for sending his posse back. His best shot at determining where he was suddenly appeared as he popped out of the brush and onto a rutted road. Going south, he figured, must lead him to Liberty, or at least a nearby mining operation. Either way, maybe he could find food and shelter before deciding whether to push on or give it up.

Just as Stevens turned south to follow the road, he could barely make out four riders, astride their still horses, well off in the distance atop a hill. A shiver went up his back. He knew they had seen him as readily as he had spotted them. And while he had no idea what they had in mind, they appeared to be watching his movements, and they weren't cowboys tending a herd of cattle, either. With all the trouble lately from renegade raiding parties, he knew in an instant he was being watched by four Apache braves.

The sheriff picked up the pace, urging his horse to a trot as he tried to keep the Indians in sight as he headed for what he hoped would be refuge. But the Indians didn't try to follow him. Instead, after his third look over his shoulder, they just seemed to disappear into thin air. Jittery from the thought of being stalked by a band of Apaches, Stevens didn't let up his pace. Exactly how much danger he might be in, he wasn't certain, but he wasn't going to hang around trying to figure it all out. He wanted to put some distance between himself and where he'd last seen the Indians.

"I knew we shoulda rode faster. Weren't no reason to wander all over hell's half acre hidin' our tracks. They found the stage before we got back, anyway. Now what're we goin' to do? What if some busybody starts speculatin' on where we were all this time, and—"

"Shut up, you fool! We got nothin' to worry about. We left nothin' out there to tie us to this. Stay calm, and everything will work out. But you gotta keep your big mouth shut, understand?" Drago gave Cloyd a withering frown as he spoke through gritted teeth.

"Uh-huh. I hope you know what you're doin'. If you was to ask me, I'd say we take our stash and light outta here tonight." Cloyd was growing increasingly nervous. He swallowed hard and looked around as if he sensed every eye in town fixed on him, certain the citizenry knew he was hiding something.

"Look, if these two men found the stagecoach and were foolish enough to bring it right back here, what's to keep us from makin' out it could have been them that done it? We can throw suspicion onto these strangers." Drago looked particularly pleased at his impromptu plan.

Cloyd grunted. "Seems to me anybody who'd do a killin' and then drop the evidence right in our lap has got to be pretty stupid—or they could prove they didn't do it. Most folks would think the same. How you gonna make out different?"

"First, we brace them, see what they know. Never you mind. I'll think of something after that."

Kelly had settled into a chair leaned against the wall in front of the general store, one of the only shady places in town, chewing on a strip of beef jerky he'd bought inside. Spotted Dog squatted beside him, doing the same. When Kelly first saw the two hard types coming down the street toward him, he took an instant dislike to both of them. He'd seen plenty of gunslingers, even in his few years as a lawman, and he knew right away that these men settled their disputes with a bullet. Something in Drago's eyes, a cold emptiness that he had seen many times before, told the young marshal to be cautious. Always before, when he'd seen that look—that look of deception that exposes men without a soul—he had learned to be ready for anything. This time would be no exception. He bit off another piece of jerky and eased his rifle closer as he watched the sheriff approach. Spotted Dog sensed Kelly's uneasiness. He, too, prepared for whatever was to come. His long, bony fingers stroked the leather-wrapped hilt of the knife stuck into his wide cloth belt.

"I hear you brought the stage in. Found it robbed and the driver and guard killed. That about the size of it?" said Drago, stopping about ten feet from where Kelly and the Indian sat, casually pulling off pieces of jerky and sipping from bottles of sarsaparilla, a taste that Spotted Dog had never experienced before. The look on the Indian's face with each drag from the bottle suggested he liked it.

"That's about it. The two dead men are at the under-taker's parlor."

"When did you come upon it?"

"About three hours ago."

"Got any notion who mighta done it?"

Just then Cloyd walked away toward where Kelly had tied up their horses. His eyes grew wide as he recognized George Alvord's horse. He hurried back to Drago's side. "Uh, Sheriff, we need to palaver." Cloyd tugged at Drago's sleeve.

Drago shrugged him off. "Not now, Cloyd. Can't you see I'm discussin' things here with, uh—come to think of it, I don't recall getting' your name, mister."

"Kelly. Piedmont Kelly."

"Kelly, huh? And who might the Injun be?"

"Don't rightly know. He don't say much."

"How long you two been ridin' together?'

"A week or so."

"And you don't even know his name?"

"Like I said, he don't say much."

Cloyd's impatience was showing a rise in urgency. He again tugged at Drago's shirt. "Sheriff, there's somethin' we should discuss right away. Maybe over at the jail."

"Cloyd, I'll be with you as soon as I'm finished here. You run along, and I'll be there shortly." He turned back to Kelly and gave a disgusted shake of his head. "Hard to find good deputies nowadays. Cloyd gets a little mulish time and again."

"If you got business elsewhere, Sheriff, don't let us hold you up."

"Well, don't the two of you go nowhere till I've had a chance to look that stagecoach over and take a gander at the bodies. We'll talk again—real soon."

"Wouldn't think of leavin' your fair town, Sheriff."

Drago nodded, then turned to head off for the jail.

Kelly leaned over to Spotted Dog. "The deputy took a keen notice of that horse you're riding. It belonged to a man named George Alvord, a man who most likely took part in the first holdup, the one your people were blamed for. He was later murdered. Seeing that horse sure did seem to upset that Cloyd fella."

Spotted Dog grunted his agreement.

On his way to the jail, Drago was stopped by a man carrying a burlap sack.

"Sheriff, would it be all right if I was to leave these eggs with you? I been up to your house to deliver them to your missus, but she don't seem to be home. Didn't want to just leave 'em sittin' in the sun," said Jerome Jones, a local farmer who supplied many of the towns-folk with fresh eggs and chickens.

"What do you mean, Flower ain't home? She's always home. Knock louder. Maybe she's nappin' or some-thin'."

"Tried that. Why, I even pushed at the door. It was open just a tad, and I called out to her loud as I dared. No answer," said Jones. "Okay if I just leave 'em with you?"

Drago grabbed the sack out of Jones' hand. "I suppose you want to be paid right here and now too."

Daunted by Drago's brusque behavior, Jones merely

turned on his heel and hurried off. "Nope. Tomorrow will do, Sheriff. Just drop it by at your convenience," Jones said over his shoulder, leaving Drago in the middle of the street, holding the bag and looking perplexed.

Shaken by the prospect of having a bunch of Apaches swoop down on his wagon, Garcia slapped the reins on the horses' rumps. The pace quickened, but Garcia's nervousness continued unabated. As he whipped the horses, trying to keep the wagon squarely in the middle of the road, where the fewest rocks might be found to jar his passenger with painful bouncing around, Garcia looked again at the place where the Indians had been, but, to his amazement, they were no longer there.

His fear that they might at that very moment be circling around for an attack nearly had his heart in his throat. He slapped at the reins and yelled to his team to keep up the pace. In the back of the wagon, Flower was being jostled pretty severely in spite of the straw Garcia had packed into the bed to cushion her journey. She groaned at each bump but was able to slowly gather her wits about her.

While she couldn't make out exactly what was happening, the voice she heard didn't belong to her husband, so she was calmed to know that Emmett had not yet found her. For that, she was thankful. As to why she was being so roughly transported to heaven knows where, she had no idea, but she was forced to accept that, for now, she could but hope for the best. Flower's ability to withstand physical punishment and stand up to adversity were her greatest assets—besides, of course, her natural beauty. Everybody said so.

After about three hours of hard driving and with his team of horses heavily lathered, Garcia saw the outskirts of Cochise. He slowed the team to cool them off. When he was safely inside the town, he came upon a couple of men walking across the street, and he called to them.

"Hey, where can I find a doctor?"

One of the men pointed to a whitewashed bungalow a few hundred feet away.

"Obliged, mister." He pulled the wagon up in front of the house, jumped down, and ran to the door. He pounded on it so hard that when the doctor yanked it open, Garcia nearly fell inside.

"Who are you? And what in tarnation is so consarned important that you have to beat my door down?" the doctor growled as he stood in the doorway, arms crossed, glasses far down on his nose, looking quite ill-tempered.

"S-sorry, sir. My name is Garcia. I run the stage stop between here and Liberty. I got a woman in the wagon what got herself burned pretty bad out in the desert. I-I didn't mean to do no damage," stammered Garcia, his hat clutched tightly to his chest.

"Well, all right, let's have a look at this woman."

The two of them carried Flower inside and placed her on a long table in the examining room. The doctor looked her over carefully, gently pulling away the cloth that Elizabeth Garcia had wrapped around her arms to prevent further exposure to the sun.

"Who put all this salve on her?"

"My wife, Elizabeth. Did she do wrong?"

"Why, no. She did a fine job. This little lady's gonna be pretty badly blistered for a few days, but she'll survive."

"That's good news, Doc. Reckon I'll take my leave, then, and saunter over to the saloon. I could use a stiff shot of whiskey," said Garcia. He quietly closed the door behind him and returned to his wagon. He figured he might just as well stay in town for the night, seeing as how it was near sundown, anyway.

"No sense givin' those redskins the same target twice in the same day," he muttered to himself.

Chapter Twenty-two

Drago seemed to be taking his sweet time, so Cloyd impatiently stuck his head out the door to see where he was. To his surprise, he saw the sheriff storming up the hill toward his own house. "Didn't he listen to me?" the deputy grumbled. Cloyd felt anger gnawing on him as he watched Drago disappear out of sight behind the feed store. "He don't never listen to me."

He had a deep foreboding about seeing Alvord's horse in the hands of the two strangers, and one of them an Apache, at that. *And now all Drago can think of is seeing Flower,* Cloyd thought, seething inside. He'd had about all he could handle of the almighty Sheriff Drago, always the one to decide everyone else's fate. *Well, maybe the time has come to change all that,* thought Cloyd. *Maybe all that money should just disappear while Drago's not around to notice.*

*   *   *

Drago slammed through the front door of his house, shouting curses as he went. "Flower, confound you, where have you made off to?"

He didn't have to look very far to realize she wasn't there; after all, there were only two real rooms, with the tiny kitchen attached, and virtually no place to hide. And why would she hide from her own husband, anyway? Hadn't he been good to her ever since he took her out of that whiskey-stinkin' saloon in Tombstone? Hadn't he given her a home, nice clothes, an easy life?

It wasn't just her absence that struck him, for she could, after all, just be downtown, gossiping with the local women. No, it was all the empty drawers, pulled out of the dresser and dumped on the floor, an obvious testament to her purposefully moving out. The wardrobe he'd had sent from Kansas City was also empty, along with all the pegs along the wall where she always hung her hats and her apron. Flower had sent him a message, and he didn't like it one bit.

"Woman! What's going on here? Where are you? If this is your idea of a joke, I ain't laughin'." He stormed out onto the small front porch and grabbed the bentwood chair he often found Flower sitting in on warm evenings. He threw the chair as far as he could, barely taking notice that it landed catawampus on the hard-packed ground and splintered into several pieces. The chair was now only fit for kindling. He stared at it angrily; then, leaving the front door wide open, he headed back to the jail in a dead run.

Cloyd saw him coming around the corner just as he was preparing to mount his horse for a quick trip to the mine to recover the stolen money and head out on his own. The decision hadn't come easy for him, but it seemed the only logical thing to do in light of Drago's recent lack of regard for the potential of getting caught and hanged for their crimes. That assumed, of course, that anyone was smart enough to tie them to the two robberies and all the killings. But he didn't put that past some clever lawman.

"Just where do you think you're goin'?" Drago said as he ran up to his deputy.

"Uh, comin' to look for you, that's all," stammered Cloyd. "What's wrong?"

"It's Flower. She's up and left."

"Maybe she's just down to the general store, gettin' somethin' she needs," said Cloyd.

"Ain't nothin' she needs, and besides, she don't take all her earthly belonging' for goin' to town." Drago spat on the ground as he said it, as if he had to get such an idea as Flower's leaving him out of his head, and the only way he could think of to do it was to spit.

The look that suddenly came over Cloyd's face made Drago grab the scruffy deputy by the shirt collar and yank hard. "What is it? You know somethin', don't you?"

"W-why no, I-I don't know nothing at all, Sheriff."

Drago yanked his six-shooter from its holster and shoved it hard into Cloyd's belly. "You got just ten seconds to spill what you know, or I'll splatter your innards all over this here street. Do you understand, you little weasel?"

"Yes, sir," Cloyd squeaked. "I seen Flower a coupla days ago down at the stage office. She looked to be buyin' a ticket to somewhere. I asked her where she was goin', but she just shoved on past me without so much as a howdy-do."

"Why didn't you tell me this before?"

"I don't rightly know. Reckon I figured you already knew. Why would she take off without tellin' you?"

Drago slowly removed the revolver from Cloyd's middle and replaced it in his holster. He began stroking his chin, a sign that something had occurred to him that he didn't like. His dark, suntanned face turned as white as a sheet.

"This isn't good news."

"What's the matter?" said Cloyd, clearly relieved to be off the hook for withholding information about Flower but increasingly fearful of whatever awful thought had struck the sheriff.

"Leave me to think this thing out, will you? We may have ourselves one serious problem."

Cloyd knew from Drago's expression that something big was brewing. He watched Drago's face seem to age ten years as they stood there. The man who had all the answers was suddenly struck dumb by some catastrophe that he had yet to reveal to his deputy.

Kelly pushed himself out of the chair, stretched, and stepped off the boardwalk.

"Spotted Dog, let's amble over to the livery. I want to find out whatever I can about Alvord's horse."

The Apache nodded and fell in behind the marshal. They took their horses' reins and led the animals down the street to Brown's Livery. They were met at the entrance by a burly man with an abundant, thick beard and bushy eyebrows that looked like small animals trained to sit there and shade his eyes from the sun.

"What can I do for you gents?"

"You Mr. Brown?" said Kelly.

"Naw. Brown got hisself drunk and was gunned down in Charleston a coupla years back. I'm the new owner, Deakins. Didn't see any point in changing the name, since I'd have to pay to have the sign repainted."

"Well, Mr. Deakins, I'd like to hear anything you can tell me about this horse," said Kelly. He led Alvord's horse forward and handed the reins to the man.

Deakins lifted the horse's right rear leg and clucked his tongue.

"Ol' Alvord sold you his horse without gettin' that shoe fixed, eh?"

"You know George Alvord?"

"Yup. Left town a couple weeks back. Ain't seen him since."

"Did he leave alone?"

"Can't rightly say. I just got up one morning, and his horse was gone. He stayed over at the Liberty Hotel. Had for several months."

"Who were his friends?"

"Well, he seemed to be on real friendly terms with

Sheriff Drago. I seen them together some. And I heard he had some kinda relative—cousin or somethin'—down in Cochise."

"Thanks for your help," said Kelly as he turned to leave.

"Say, where is ol' Alvord?"

"Boot Hill," said Kelly over his shoulder.

The doctor at Cochise looked in on Flower as she slept fitfully. She uttered a weak groan as she tried to get comfortable. When residents heard that a woman had been found on the road, badly dehydrated and burned from the sun, only one lady volunteered to help out. Nettie. She called on the doctor with a basket of fresh rolls and a vase filled with cheery flowers.

"Good morning, Miss Nettie," said the doctor as he opened the door to his office. "What brings you by?"

"I hear you have a guest who could use some cheering up. I would like to do whatever I can to help."

The doctor stepped aside and waved her in. "I'd be grateful for an extra hand, ma'am."

The doctor led the way to where Flower was lying in the doctor's own bed. He went to her side, lifted a cold compress from her face, and dipped it into a bowl of water on a nightstand beside the bed. As he wrung it out in preparation to replace it across her burned eyelids, Nettie let out a gasp.

"Oh, my! It's . . . uh, t-terrible. . . ."

"Yes, she's been pretty badly burned from exposure to the sun's direct rays. But it's actually not as serious as it looks. Garcia got her here in quick order, and his wife had the good sense to bathe her in horse salve. She'll be up and around soon with no ill effects after some rest," he said.

"Has she . . . said anything?"

"Not a word. And I find no reason other than that she just doesn't want to. Fear of strange people and strange places, perhaps. I can't really say. But if you'd like, you can sit with her for a spell. I have another patient due any time now. Call out if you need me," said the doctor as he closed the door behind him.

As soon as she was certain she wouldn't be heard, she whispered, "Flower. It's me, Nettie. What happened to you?"

Flower stirred at the sound of a familiar voice. She winced as she tugged at the compress covering her eyes. At the sight of Nettie, she blinked, then broke into tears. She tried to rise but fell back, whimpering.

"Flower, what happened? How did you end up lying in the road, near burned to a crisp with sunstroke?"

"I-I was runnin' away from Emmett. And he'll kill me for sure if he finds me. Please don't tell anyone I'm here. Word will surely get back to him if you do," whispered Flower.

"I won't tell anyone—don't you worry. But why were you running away? Didn't the two of you get hitched? That's what I heard from one of the other girls, anyway."

"Yeah, but if that was what bein' married means, I don't want any more of it. He beat me somethin' awful whenever he'd get a snootful of red-eye. Sometimes I couldn't get out of bed for two days after he'd come home drunk, mean, and needin' someone to take a beatin'. That was my wifely duty, I reckon. Well, I've had all I can take of that kind of duty."

"Oh, my goodness, Flower, I'm so sorry you had to put up with such awful treatment, but working that saloon wasn't any picnic, either. Drunken cowboys tearing at our clothes, treating us like some kind of merchandise," said Nettie with a shake of her head. "I had my fill of *that* too."

"That why you settled down here in Cochise?" asked Flower.

"This is a nice quiet town, and people treat you like you was normal folk. 'Course, they don't know where I came from, either."

"You didn't tell anyone?"

"Nope. I just tell 'em my husband died some time back. When they think you're a widow woman, they pretty much quit asking questions. So you can be certain your secret is safe with me. And as soon as you feel up to it, you come right on over and stay with me. I got plenty of room."

Flower reached over and took Nettie's hand. "Thank you. I feel safer already."

"If you saw Flower buyin' a ticket on the stage, and she ain't here, then what's that tell you?"

"I reckon she left on the stage. That what you figure?" said Cloyd.

"But you said no one got onto the stage."

"Yeah. That's right. So how could she have been on it?"

"She musta met it outside of town, you idiot. And if she was on the stage when we robbed it, she can identify us. This is serious!"

"Maybe I *shoulda* looked, huh?" Cloyd said sarcastically.

Drago started pacing nervously. "We gotta find her. She's out there somewhere. Those men that brought the stage in didn't mention seein' any passengers, so . . ."

"Oh, yeah, I almost forgot to tell you. One of them was ridin' George's horse. How do you suppose he come by that ol' mare, anyway?"

Chapter Twenty-three

"If he's got Alvord's horse, where's Alvord? And what happened to his share of the money them two took with them? You don't suppose these boys got it, do you?" Drago shouted.

"How would I know? I cain't even figure out how they got the horse in the first place."

"The *horse!* That's it! We'll get them for horse-stealin', and I'll lock 'em up till I can get Flower back here. With her home, she wouldn't dare say nothin' about us bein' in on the robbery. She knows I'd cut her good," said Drago as an evil grin swept across his face.

Cloyd liked the idea too, though he was still harboring thoughts about how he could get his hands on all the money they had stashed and skedaddle out of town. But the success of any such plans were fading, as it looked

191

like Drago wasn't intending on letting him out of his sight anytime soon.

The two of them hurried to the general store where they'd last seen Kelly and the Indian. When they found they weren't there, Drago began to sweat profusely, and not from the heat, either. He had no idea who these strangers were, but he needed them to set his plan into motion, a plan that would keep him above suspicion in the robbery and killings, either of which charge could get him hanged. He'd seen too many men end their days at the end of a rope, and he wasn't eager to join their ranks.

Just then Cloyd spotted the two strangers ambling down the street toward them.

"Here they come, Sheriff, walkin' right into our hands, easy as you please."

Drago met Kelly and Spotted Dog in the middle of the street and quickly drew his gun. "Well, gents, if you'll just shed your weapons and hand them over to my deputy, we'll take us a little walk to the jail, where you'll be spendin' a few days."

"What is the charge, Sheriff?" said Kelly, frowning as he obliged by unbuckling his belt.

"Horse-stealin' for starters," said Drago. "Then we'll look into this stage robbery. Maybe you two ain't as innocent as you'd have folks believe."

Cloyd quickly took the Winchester from Kelly's hand, as well as his gun belt and Colt. Spotted Dog wasn't carrying a gun, so Cloyd just shrugged and, with arms full, led the way to the jail. When they got there, Drago pushed Kelly and the Indian into the first cell and locked the door.

"That'll keep you till I can figure out where you got that stolen horse and whether you were in on the stage robbery," said Drago.

Kelly could keep his tongue no longer. "What makes you think we stole a horse, Sheriff?" he said.

"Because it belongs to a friend of mine, name of George Alvord, that's how. And I know he wouldn't sell it."

"That's true, I didn't buy it, but I'm pretty sure the owner doesn't need it anymore, since he's well past caring."

"Yeah? Well, just what does that mean?"

"Mr. Alvord is dead."

"What! How did it happen? You shoot him?"

"No, I didn't shoot him. He died in his sleep, with a little help from a sharp blade."

"Say, how do you know all this?"

"I was nearby when it happened."

"If you was close and you didn't do it, then you must know who did," said Drago.

"I have no idea. I was just gonna ask you the same thing," said Kelly.

"How should I know? I wasn't there. You can just settle in here until I figure all this out."

"Is your deputy gonna stay behind and keep an eye on us while you're out checkin' our story, Sheriff? We will need food, and all." Kelly said it quite nonchalantly as he settled down on one end of the cell's only cot. Spotted Dog squatted on the floor, leaning against a wall, his hand covering the hilt of the knife that Cloyd had missed.

Drago thought about leaving Cloyd behind. He saw an opportunity to take the cash and leave town. But then, he still needed to find Flower. If he could locate her, he could not only keep her from testifying against him, but he could also force her to give him an alibi, since the dead stage driver and the guard were the only ones who knew she'd been onboard.

Cloyd saw that Drago was mired in a serious quandary and decided to jump in. "Don't you never mind who'll be keepin' watch over you fellas. The liveryman, Deakins, has a shotgun that'll keep you quiet till we get back. Ain't that right, Sheriff?"

"Uh, yeah. Cloyd, you go get Deakins and tell him he's goin' to get deputized for a spell."

Sheriff John Henry Stevens was awakened more by a strange feeling he had than by the sun breaking over the horizon and hitting him squarely in the face. He'd had to bed down in the desert beneath an overhanging boulder, the only shelter he could find from the blowing sands of the oncoming storm. It was something he hated doing, because the ground was hard and had more than its share of things that liked to crawl around in the dark, many of them poisonous. Fortunately, it had remained a dry storm, sending thousands of bolts of lightning to earth through the highly charged, dry air, but not a drop of water fell. For that, he was thankful, as he had neither slicker nor poncho to protect him.

As he yawned and opened his eyes, he was met with a sight that would have struck fear into the heart of any man. There, staring down at him, stood four Chiricahua Apaches, motionless and without expression, wearing bloodred headbands and high moccasins.

"Wh-what!" John Henry jumped to his feet while at the same time trying without success to extricate his sidearm, which, to his surprise, was no longer in its holster. He swallowed hard as he blinked to clear his vision. Then one of the Indians smiled, and the four of them stepped back a few feet. That's when the sheriff recognized them as the ones who had sprung Spotted Dog from his jail in Cochise. He also noticed his revolver lying atop his saddle several feet from where he had been sleeping. He hadn't put it there, so it was clear the Indians had removed it in order that he not start shooting when he awakened, before he could think clearly. *This is the second time I've awakened to Indians staring down at me, and I don't like it one bit. Maybe I'm gettin' too old for this job.*

"What are you doing here? I thought the marshal told you to go back to San Carlos," Stevens sputtered.

One of them spoke up in a mixture of pidgin English and hand signs.

"We follow the white eyes. Find men who kill our people."

"Yeah, well, I don't reckon I blame you none, after

what we found out there near that rimrock, but we ain't caught up to them yet. We think the same men robbed another one of our stagecoaches and killed two more men. I'm tryin' to track them now."

"We help."

Stevens thought about that for a moment. He wasn't entirely comfortable keeping company with four members of one of the deadliest Indian peoples on the frontier. But with four other sets of eyes and the tracking skills that came with them, maybe it wasn't such a far-fetched idea at that. Besides, if they'd intended to kill him, they'd already had more than enough opportunities.

"All right, boys, you can get started by helpin' me find the tracks they left, so we can see where they got to. The last I seen of their trail was over there yonder, just where the dry creek bed turns to solid granite."

The sheriff couldn't be certain whether the Apaches understood more than a handful of his words, but without hesitation they spread out and began combing the area for any hint of where the outlaws had gone.

In only minutes, one of the scouts let out a whoop, and they all ran to see what he had discovered. Sure enough, the outlaws' tracks were once again visible after several hundred feet of sandy gravel and granite creek bed. They had obviously decided to get to higher ground, although Stevens could see no logic to this move, as the creek meandered for better than a mile farther before returning to a sandy bottom. It looked as if they were headed for a specific location, either to hide out or secrete their booty for their later return. But why not just keep going?

As John Henry rode slowly along, trying to watch the ground for a hint of where the outlaws were headed, the Apaches spread out, weaving back and forth through the brush and cacti to be sure they weren't following a false trail. As they came to a series of hills, John Henry noticed a number of piles of tailings, useless rock left over from the mining process. *An old mine would be a good place to hide stolen money,* he thought, and he pushed on, keeping an eye out for an opening or some clue to recent activity. All five of them converged on one location at the same time. The entrance to the abandoned mine was protected from view by a number of trees and shrubs fed by water trickling out of the mine's mouth and a small nearby creek.

They dismounted and slowly approached the mouth of the tunnel. Stevens said nothing, merely giving hand signals to the Indians to follow him. He pulled his pistol and cocked the hammer. The Indians, armed with rifles, did the same. The sound sent a shiver up the sheriff's back as he thought of proceeding into a darkened, abandoned mineshaft with four armed Apaches behind him.

But Sheriff Stevens was doomed to disappointment. Upon finding a lantern with sufficient coal oil in it to afford some light, he found no tracks inside the tunnel. "Well, it surely does look like this ain't the place. I coulda swore we was on the right trail."

One of the Indians pointed to his nose. "Death," he said.

Stevens cocked his head and frowned in disbelief. "You sayin' someone been killed here?"

The Indian grunted and took the lantern from Stevens' hand. He started down the tunnel. The others followed, with the sheriff now bringing up the rear. As they wound around to where the tunnel split, the Indian instinctively followed the shaft as it turned to the right. They had gone only about twenty yards when the scout stopped and pointed to a newly mounded pile of dirt. Stevens shoved ahead and began pulling dirt away with his hands. When he uncovered Devlin's corpse, the face bleached white, with a hole in the forehead, he jumped back, nearly gagging at the smell.

"Well, I'll be . . . you was right, Injun. Looks like we got us a killin', even if we don't have evidence of a hideout. But someone had to have been in here. This fella didn't commit suicide, then cover himself up."

Without an extra horse or anything to wrap the body in, Stevens left the corpse in the shallow grave and led the four scouts back outside. "I'll go to Liberty and tell the sheriff about this. You fellas best not come into town with me. Someone might just get the wrong idea."

The Apaches nodded their understanding, mounted up, and soon disappeared into the brush.

When Sheriff Stevens rode into Liberty an hour later, he headed straight for Drago's office. As he pushed open the door, he found the liveryman, Deakins, leaning back in the desk chair, feet up on an open drawer, sound asleep.

"Hey, Deputy, where's Sheriff Drago?"

Deakins jumped at the sound of a voice and, blinking

to adjust to the light, stood up abruptly. "Why, er, he's gone to look for where them stage robbers might have stashed their ill-gotten gains, so we'll have the evidence to hang 'em for the murder of the driver and his guard."

"So, the stage was robbed. You mean you already caught the low-down lizards that done it?" The surprise on Stevens' face at hearing there had been two more murders turned to an angry frown. "Where are they?"

"We got 'em right back yonder in a cell. Want to take a look for yourself?"

"I'd be obliged," said Stevens as he followed Deakins to the back.

Steven's expression turned from anger to shock as he came face-to-face with Drago's two prisoners.

Chapter Twenty-four

"Where we headin', Sheriff?" said Cloyd as they cut cross-country out of the livery's back corral about an hour before Stevens rode into town.

"First, we find Flower and shut her up. We'll go to where we left the stagecoach and see if we can pick up her trail. She couldn't have got far in all this heat."

"The relay station's only about seven miles on farther—maybe she made it there," said Cloyd.

"Then we'll just have to look in on Garcia and his wife if we don't find her aforehand. I hope they don't know nothin', 'cause I don't want to have to kill them too."

They urged their mounts to a trot toward the curve in the road where they had murdered the stage driver and the guard. Drago was growing increasingly nervous and shaken by the possibility that Flower might have made her way to someone for help and already told what she knew about the robbery and shootings.

"She not only had to survive the heat of the day, but she had to find someplace to hole up last night. Some of them critters out there wouldn't mind findin' a helpless woman wanderin' through their territory." Cloyd grinned.

" 'Course, if we find her first, it don't make no never mind if she is helpless. She's gonna be givin' us an alibi or get dead," growled Drago.

"Couldn't we just try to talk some sense into her? She don't have to die if we get her to listen to reason, does she?"

"You do sound like you're sweet on Flower. That right? You smitten with my pretty little wife?"

"Aw, no, Drago. Nothin' like that. Why, I wouldn't carry no feelin's for another man's woman, 'specially not yours. I'm just thinkin' it'd be a shame to kill her for just bein' on that stage where she shouldn't oughta been, that's all," said Cloyd.

"Uh-huh. I'll still bet you was over at my house that day tryin' to talk a little sweet-talk to her. Cloyd, if you weren't so darn dumb, I'd plug you."

"I wasn't there for no such reason. You can believe me or not, but I wouldn't do such a thing behind your back. Why, I thought we was friends. Friends don't act that way."

*   *   *

Flower's stumbling tracks were easy to follow, but they led to where several horses had stopped. Then all signs of her stopped too. A cold sweat rolled off Drago's brow as he realized she'd been found and by now had probably already talked her fool head off. He and Cloyd were dead men if they didn't just grab the loot and head for California or New Mexico straightaway.

But the idea of having to be on the run all because of a mouthy woman didn't set right with Drago. A strong desire to get revenge was building fast and filling his head with a risky plan. Besides, with her out of the way, who'd be left to testify against them in court?

Cloyd just stood stone still right where Flower had stumbled. He kept shaking his head and mumbling, "This ain't good, Drago. This ain't good."

"Shut up, you fool. Cain't you see I'm thinkin'?"

"But what's there to think about? We may be only hours away from bein' on the wrong end of a length of hemp, and that don't appeal to me. I say we hightail it outta here, pronto."

"We ain't goin' nowhere till I say so," growled Drago. He pulled his revolver and aimed it at Cloyd's head. "And if you don't like that, I'll end your worryin' right here and now."

"I-I'm with you, Drago. Whatever you say is fine by me." Cloyd was shaking so badly, he couldn't have drawn on the sheriff if he even dared to, which he didn't. At least not right then.

Drago jammed the Colt back into his holster, stroked his stubbly chin for a minute, then grunted an acknowledgment that he'd come to a conclusion. "Okay, let's ride for Garcia's place."

"What is goin' on here, Deputy? Why do you have a United States Marshal locked up in jail?" yelled Stevens.

Deakins was wide-eyed at the revelation. "A marshal? I-I don't know anything about a marshal. Sheriff Drago locked them two up for horse-stealin' and maybe havin' somethin' to do with the stagecoach holdup," sputtered Deakins.

"Well, get the key, and let them outta there, you idiot! And be quick about it. They had nothin' to do with either one of them things."

"Yes, sir, Sheriff," said Deakins as he fumbled with the desk drawer where a ring with three keys was kept. He rushed back and began stabbing at the keyhole, succeeding in releasing the lock only after three tries. "I-I am very sorry, sir. I had no idea you was a marshal. I just done what Drago told me."

"It's all right, Mister Deakins. I know what happened." Kelly stepped from the cell, followed closely by Spotted Dog, who had been none too happy to be locked in a jail cell again. He'd had all the white man's confinement he could handle during the past few days.

After retrieving his rifle and sidearm, Kelly, along with Stevens and the Indian, stepped outside. Kelly motioned for Spotted Dog to find their horses.

"What's goin' on here, Marshal? Why'd Drago put you two behind bars?" Stevens said.

"He didn't know I was a marshal because I kept that

piece of information hidden from him. On purpose." He pulled the badge from his pocket and pinned it to his shirt. "I wanted to see his reaction when he spotted Alvord's horse."

"What'd he do?"

"He was nervous, jittery. Seemed to want to get us out of the way while he left town on the premise of looking into the stage robbery. But he never asked any questions about where we found the stagecoach. I got the feelin' he already knew that. Since we didn't tell anyone, how could he have known without bein' involved somehow?"

"Sounds like you figure to tie him to both robberies. That right?" said Stevens.

"He's sure actin' strange for a lawman who says he's intent on gettin' answers to a crime—more like a man tryin' to divert suspicion from himself. Say, where'd you come from? I thought you went back with the lady."

"I did. We took her to the Garcia place. Elizabeth Garcia is good at tending to them in need—folks or animals. She'll do whatever's necessary to help that poor thing get better. I sent the others on back to Cochise."

"I'm glad you decided to come lookin' for us. We mighta been sittin' in here for a spell. At least until I pulled my badge on poor ol' Deakins."

"Well, I didn't come straight here. I followed the tracks of the varmints that done the robbery and killin'," said Stevens. "Spent a miserable night dodgin' lightnin' bolts too, then got scared near outta my wits when I awoke this mornin'."

"What happened?"

"I come eyeball to eyeball with them four savages Spotted Dog told to skedaddle back to the reservation, that's what. Near put me in my grave."

"Did they say why they were there?"

"Wanted to help find the ones who killed their people. They figured it was the same ones that robbed the stage and killed the driver and guard. Offered to help me track 'em."

"And where did the tracks lead?"

"Well, they led to an old mine shaft that's been played out for years, but there weren't no tracks leadin' in nor out. Oh, yeah, I almost forgot. We went inside and found a corpse in there. Been dead a couple days, I figure," said Stevens. "So, what do you figure on doin' now, Marshal?"

"We're goin' back to that mine."

As the three of them mounted up, Kelly turned to Spotted Dog and said, "You didn't tell your friends to go back to San Carlos, did you? Probably said to keep a close eye on us."

The old Apache just looked away without comment.

"Well, miss, you are going to be very sore for a few days, but I think the worst is over," said the doctor. "The blisters will heal slowly, but you must keep putting this salve on every day so there won't be any permanent damage."

"Thank you, Doctor."

"Here I've been tending you for a couple of days, and I don't even know your name, child."

"My name? Uh, my name is, uh, Abigail, uh, S-Smith," she stuttered.

"I can see by that ring on your finger that you're a married lady. I should send word to your husband that you are here and safe," said the doctor.

"No! Oh, please, whatever you do, please don't let him know I'm here. He'll kill me."

"I'm sure you're exaggerating. He might be a little put out that you were wandering around in the desert without even a hat or an umbrella, but I'm sure he'd stop short of killing you, my dear," the doctored said, chuckling at the thought.

"You don't understand. If he finds me, he *will* kill me, and for reasons I can't explain. Just don't say a word to anyone about who or where I am. Please, I beg you," Flower said. Tears flowed down her cheeks.

"All right. If that's the way you wish it, I'll not say anything. I reckon I couldn't locate him without your help, anyway. So you just lie back and get some rest. I'll look in on you later."

Just then Nettie appeared at the doctor's door with a covered basket. "Good morning, Doctor. I brought some fresh biscuits and prickly pear jam to help cheer your patient," said Nettie.

"Certainly, Miss Nettie. Please go on back. I'm sure she'll enjoy your visit. She could use some cheering up. I must leave to see how Mrs. Barker's baby is coming along."

When Nettie entered Flower's room, she noticed immediately that Flower had been crying.

"What's the matter, Flower? Doc says you'll be healed up in no time at all."

"Nettie, I got more problems than a few blisters. My life is over. I'm a dead woman if Emmett finds me," said Flower, visibly shaken, nervously wrapping and unwrapping a handkerchief around her fingers.

"Goodness, gracious, Flower, Drago isn't going to kill you just for running away. Why, they'd hang him in a flash."

"It ain't that. It's for what I saw."

"What in heaven's name are you talking about?"

"I was on that stage to Cochise. I heard you lived here now, and I was coming to find you. But the stage was robbed. The driver and guard were killed. I heard it all. I know who did it."

"That's just awful, Flower. You poor thing. But how come you weren't killed too?"

"They didn't know I was inside the coach. They didn't even look. I was hidin' under the seat and didn't come out till they had gone. Then I started walkin' down the road to get as far away as possible before he found out I was on that stage." Flower rolled over and buried her face in the pillow, sobbing uncontrollably.

Nettie reached out and laid a hand on Flower's back. She patted her gently. "If you know who the robbers are, Flower, you have to tell the sheriff. He'll be back soon, I'm sure."

"Back? Wh-where is he?"

"He and a United States Marshal left to find out why

the stage was overdue. I guess we now know why, don't we? So, who *did* do the killing?"

"It was Emmett and that awful deputy, Cloyd."

"What! You're saying your own husband is a thief *and* a murderer?" Nettie said, aghast and shaken at what she was hearing.

"I'm so ashamed. I was livin' with a man like that, and I never even knew it."

"Well, it wasn't your fault you didn't know before you were married that he was a rattlesnake. And a killer. Does anyone else know what you've just told me?" said Nettie.

"I, uh, asked the doctor not to let my husband know I'm here. I gave him a name I just made up on the spur of the moment." Flower sobbed. "What if he figures out who I really am? Emmett will be scouring the country-side."

"It's too late to worry about that, now; you've got to pull yourself together. We have to get you out of here and over to my place, where you'll be safer. Do you think you can make it?"

"I'll try."

"You'll do more than try; you'll do it. If Drago finds you, more than likely he'll kill us both. And we both know why."

Chapter Twenty-five

As Drago and Cloyd neared the Garcia ranch and relay station, they found Elizabeth outside hanging the
wash on the line. They rode up slowly and dismounted.
As she came around the building to greet them, Drago
removed his hat before addressing her.

"Howdy, Miz Garcia. Do you remember me? I'm
Sheriff Emmett Drago from over in Liberty. This here's
my deputy. We're lookin' for a woman mighta got lost
out in the desert. Do you happen to know anythin' about
her?"

"Goodness, yes. The woman you're speakin' of was
brought in yesterday all burnt up and gaspin' for water.
Poor thing had laid out there in that blisterin' sun for a
spell, I reckon."

"Who brought her in?"

"Why, it was the sheriff and a couple of men from Cochise."

"Did she mention anythin' about the stagecoach bein' held up? Did she say who she was?" Drago had a hard time containing his nervousness and began fidgeting with his belt buckle.

"Oh, my heavens. I didn't know about any stage holdup, neither. Why, that poor child couldn't get a word out, her lips were so blistered. Antonio took her into Cochise, where they got a doctor who could tend to her properly. I hope she makes it."

"You mean she could die?"

"I've seen more'n one die from heatstroke and a blisterin' burn. An' she had all that, sure 'nough, and more," said Elizabeth.

Drago was relieved that Mrs. Garcia didn't seem to know who the woman in the desert was, but now he was faced with the prospect of locating Flower and either killing her or spiriting her out of town. And by now she could have spilled everything to the Cochise sheriff and a doctor to boot. Panic was settling in. Even though his head was spinning with thoughts of what might happen when they rode into town to find Flower, Drago did remember to tip his hat as he and Cloyd mounted up and headed for Cochise.

Cloyd couldn't help but notice a change come over the expression of the cold, calculating man he thought he knew. After several miles of hard riding, Cloyd could no longer contain his curiosity as to what they hoped to accomplish by dragging Flower out of Cochise, if she was even still there.

"Drago, I don't mean to rile you none, but why don't we just get the money and light outta the county, maybe head for Santa Fe?"

"I gotta square things with that woman. It's her that got us into this situation. Why, if she'd stayed home like she was s'posed to, we could already be drinkin' tequila in some nice place in New Mexico."

"You mean us takin' a chance on gettin' hanged for them robberies and killin's is just for revenge on Flower? That don't make sense. I don't aim to dangle from a rope 'cause you want Flower to pay." Cloyd yanked back on the reins, stopping his horse in the middle of the road.

Drago went on for a bit, then stopped and turned around. His hand fell close to the butt of his six-shooter as, with a menacing glower, he stared his scruffy deputy straight in the eye. "You got two choices, and only two. Either you and I ride into Cochise together, or I bury your body right here. Make up your mind fast, 'cause I'm either leavin' in one minute, or I'm pluggin' you so full of holes, you'll whistle as you fall."

Cloyd had come to a crossroads, and he knew it. Could he outdraw Drago or not? He'd thought many times about how he'd react if given a chance like this to prove himself. It was now or never, and time was running out. One slip, and he was a dead man. Sweat began to run down his forehead and into his eyes. He was suddenly aware of just how hot the day had become, and suddenly he was conscious, too, of the far-off cry of some poor critter that had just met its end. Drago's hand inched closer to his Colt.

"Uh, okay, I-I'm with you," stammered Cloyd as he lifted his fingers away from his own sidearm and crossed his hands on the pommel.

Drago said nothing as he wheeled his horse around and spurred him to a run. Cloyd followed—immediately after wiping the sweat from his face with his handkerchief and giving a sigh of relief.

"C'mon, Flower. Get out of that bed, and help me gather up your things. I'm taking you to my place. You can hide there until this blows over—or until they catch Emmett Drago and hang him like they should have years ago," said Nettie.

Painfully Flower pulled herself up and began to dress. She still had all her undergarments on, but pulling her gingham dress over her head quickly reminded her of the ordeal she'd been through. Nettie hastily helped gather up Flower's belongings.

"I wish Marshal White hadn't stopped you from shootin' Emmett back in Tombstone after he killed your man, Colson. Funny, at the time I was scared to death you was goin' to hit him after all those shots you took, and now . . ." said Flower.

"I'd probably still be in prison if I'd hit him. I thought I'd never be able to look another lawman in the eye after White pushed me aside and took my gun away from me. I hated Emmett Drago for murdering Colson, yes, but I was also awful sore at the marshal for not arresting him. Until now, I had no use for lawmen."

"Sounds like you've had a change of mind."

"There's a U.S. Marshal in town that I guess I wouldn't mind getting to know better," said Nettie with a demure smile. "Seems a lot different from any I've known before."

"Maybe he can help me. Do you think he could take Emmett?"

"I don't know about that, but he and the sheriff left yesterday, and they haven't come back. Now, hurry. We'll leave by the back. My house is just down the alley."

Flower's nervousness resurfaced as she heard there were no lawmen in town. She imagined Emmett and Cloyd just waltzing down First Street, snatching her up, and riding out as if they were going on a picnic. She shuddered as she envisioned herself lying in a heap alongside the road, dead as could be, no more than dinner for the buzzards.

Looking in both directions to make sure they weren't seen, Flower and Nettie hurried away from the doctor's office, reaching the back of Nettie's bungalow in minutes. As they went inside, Nettie hastily drew the drapes at all of the windows so no one could see inside.

"You can take my room, Flower. I'll sleep on the floor. I'll bring food home so you won't have to go out. Now, you get settled, and I'll be back after I serve lunch at the restaurant."

Flower dropped into a chair with a sigh of relief. "Thanks, Nettie."

"It's a good feeling to be able to help an old friend."

"Someday I'll make it up to you. I only hope your takin' me in doesn't bring that devil down on us both," said Flower.

Marshal Kelly and Sheriff Stevens arrived at the mouth of the mine where the Indians had discovered the body of the murdered man buried in a shallow grave. They dismounted and glanced around to be sure they were alone. Before going inside, Kelly began searching for any evidence that Drago had been there. He found nothing unusual except a recently cut branch from a nearby cottonwood. Some of the leaves, though wilted, were covered with a bluish stain.

"I think I know why you found no tracks leadin' from the mine, John Henry. I'd say they used that branch to sweep away any footprints. Not a bad idea, either."

"What makes you think that?"

"That branch didn't cut itself down, and those stains came from that trickle of water from inside, probably full of copper sulfate."

"Copper what?"

"Copper sulfate. It leaches into the water from deposits of copper inside. I noticed Drago's boots were stained the same way when he met us on the street."

"Well, I'll be a flop-eared mule. I never knew that—about the copper, I mean."

The three of them cautiously entered the main shaft, with Stevens in the lead. He retrieved the lantern he'd used when he and the four Apache scouts discovered the body. After taking several twists and turns, they came into a room with a stack of timbers and a partially dismantled mound of dirt.

"That's him, all pasty white and startin' to smell something awful," said Stevens.

Kelly bent down to survey the corpse. "From the looks of things, I'd say he'd been doin' a little prospectin'. His pick and a chisel are lying there by that pile of stone."

"Why do you figure they shot him?"

"Maybe he found somethin' he shouldn't have. Let's look around."

All three of them began searching for a place to hide something valuable. When Spotted Dog squatted down to look over the pile of timbers, he noticed something strange.

"Wood old but still wet on top. Been moved."

Kelly and Stevens began to lift each timber off the pile and move it aside. After only four of them had been moved, three large saddlebags were revealed, resting in a cavity formed by the way the timbers had been stacked.

"Looks like we just came across someone's hiding place."

The marshal opened one of the flaps. He couldn't help but whistle when he saw all the money inside. Looking over the marshal's shoulder, Sheriff Stevens was equally astounded at what he saw.

"Must be thousands in there. But there wasn't that much money on the stage they just robbed."

"We're also lookin' at the money stolen from the first robbery—or at least some of it," said Kelly. "Look, here are some letters dated about two days before the first holdup."

"You still think Drago had something to do with all this?"

"Yes, I do. Drago, Cloyd, Alvord, and one other."

"Who do you figure the fourth one is?" said Stevens.

"I don't know yet. But I'll find him—you can bet on that."

"Maybe we ought to take the money and get it to a bank where we can count it out, make sure it's all here. The bank in Liberty is as good as any, I reckon," said Stevens.

Arriving in Liberty, their first stop was the bank. Stevens stayed there to help with counting and identifying the loot. Kelly and Spotted Dog went to the sheriff's office, looking for Drago. But when they got there, the liveryman, Deakins, was still the only one around.

"Drago been back?" said Kelly.

"No, and I'm gettin' awful tired of just sittin' here. I got work to do at my place. Say, since you're a *real* lawman, why don't you keep a watch on things whilst I go fetch some dinner and get back to cleanin' out the stalls? Would that be all right with you?"

"Go ahead, Mr. Deakins. I'll take the reins till Drago gets back."

After Deakins left, Kelly turned to Spotted Dog and said, "You are free to go. It's obvious you had nothin' to do with any robbery. I am grateful for the help you've given me."

"Same ones kill my people that kill your people?"

"Yes. It looks that way."

"I stay, then."

Kelly didn't like the look that came over the old Indian when he heard that the local sheriff might have been involved in killing both white men and red men. There was a definite thirst for revenge in the eyes of the aging Apache, a man who had seen the white man's law treat his people differently than their own. *Yes,* thought Kelly, *this old man wants to wait around to see if we are honorable in carrying out justice when it involves another white man.*

Kelly would keep a watchful eye, because, while Spotted Dog was an old man, he was still every inch an Apache. And that alone made him dangerous.

Chapter Twenty-six

"There's the doctor's office. We'll just ride around back so as not to attract a lot of attention," said Drago.

The two rode down an alley between First and Second Streets, where the livery and several saloons were located. They rode until they saw a small DOCTOR'S OFFICE sign over the back door of a whitewashed, clapboard-sided building in the middle of the block. Drago went past it and dismounted several buildings down.

Cloyd followed suit. "What are we stoppin' here for? Ain't the doctor's place a few houses down from here?"

"Yeah, but we don't want to warn him we're comin' for a visit. First we need to find out if the good doctor is inside. If we're lucky, he'll be out somewhere tendin' to healin' business, and Flower will be alone in there," said Drago.

"You want I should go peek in a window and get the lay of the land?"

"Yeah, that's a good idea, Cloyd. Go ahead."

Cloyd wrapped the reins around a fence picket and slipped between two buildings where he could sidle up close enough to the doctor's office to size up the situation without being seen. When he reached a window in the back, he hoisted himself up onto an overturned bucket and peered inside. When he heard several horses coming, Cloyd jumped off the bucket and ducked behind a fence alongside an adjoining building.

Drago looked the other way, pretending to tighten his cinch straps as the riders approached. He then mounted his horse and acted as if he were about to ride away. After the riders had passed, he dismounted again and went looking for Cloyd.

"Did you see her?" Drago whispered as he neared where Cloyd was hunkered down behind the fence.

"Didn't appear to be no one inside. I looked in both windows too."

"Hmm. Where do you suppose she could have got to? I'm goin' in."

Drago burst through the back door, finding himself in a room with glass-fronted cabinets, a long table, and dozens of bottles and medical instruments lying about. A bookshelf nearly covered one wall. He stormed through the office, sticking his head into each of the rooms. The second room was the bedroom, and someone had been lying in the bed recently. There were flowers on a side table, and a bowl with water and a damp cloth carefully folded beside it.

"She's been here. Someone's taken her out. But who, and where'd she get off to?" Drago grumbled as he stormed back out the rear door to where Cloyd was holding the horses.

"We can't go ask the sheriff, can we?" said Cloyd.

"No, you fool, but we *can* head for a saloon and ask some questions. Someone might know somethin'. Just remember, we don't give out our names in case she's been blabbin' to the locals. And put that tin badge in your pocket so they don't start askin' questions about who we are."

Cloyd did as he was told, and they tied their horses to a hitching rail in front of the first saloon they came to, the Gold Mine, and went inside. There were only three other men sitting at a table, tossing back shots of whiskey. The bartender was leaning on the bar, reading a copy of the local newspaper. Drago and Cloyd moved to the bar and ordered beers.

After they were served, Drago struck up a conversation with the bartender. "I hear there was an injured lady brought into town yesterday."

The bartender folded the newspaper and laid it aside. "That's what I hear. Don't know much about it other than they say she might have been on the stage that hasn't made it here yet. Figure it musta busted a wheel or something. The sheriff and a U.S. Marshal are out lookin' for it right now."

"Do they have any idea what happened to it?"

"Not that I've heard. Doc Reynolds took the woman in and is tendin' to her. They say she was in pretty bad shape from lyin' in the sun all day."

"Have you seen the doctor today?"

"Not yet, but he's due any time now for his regular whiskey."

Two more men entered the saloon, and the bartender moved down the bar to serve them. Drago and Cloyd each dropped a coin next to their empty glasses and wandered outside to sit on a bench and wait for someone who looked like a doctor to come by.

"It don't sound like word of the robbery has gotten here yet," said Cloyd. "So maybe Flower ain't blabbed nothin' about it."

"Uh-huh. She better not, if she knows what's good for her."

After about an hour, a buggy drove into town, stopping in front of a building with the sign that read: DOCTOR AMBROSE REYNOLD'S MEDICAL CLINIC. Drago and Cloyd ran across the dusty street to meet the well-dressed man who got out and hooked a rope with a lead weight to the horse's harness and dropped it to the ground. Before he could go inside, however, Drago was behind him with his gun drawn.

"You the doctor?"

"Why, uh, yes. Why do you ask?"

"We need to see the lady that was brought in yesterday."

"I-I'm afraid she's not here." The doctor remembered well the admonition Flower had made to him about her husband not finding her.

"Yeah, I know. We already been through your place. So, where is she?"

"I . . . I can't say I have any idea. She was here when I left. She, uh, must have . . ."

"You didn't know she was gone, did you, Doc?"

"No, I'm afraid I didn't."

"Where could she have gone? She got friends around here?"

"N-not that I know of. I got the impression she was from elsewhere." The doctor was flustered both by knowing he might be talking to someone the woman had a deadly fear of and by having a gun pointed at him.

"You got about ten seconds to come up with a name, or else *you'll* be needin' a doc yourself. Understand?" The look on the gunman's face left the doctor with no doubt as to his future if he didn't comply. Time was running out for him to decide his fate. It took little imagination to figure out that his patient had gone with Nettie, the only person who had visited the stricken woman, and a woman for whom he also had great regard.

At just that moment Nettie closed the door to the restaurant almost directly across the street and started for her house with an armload of food. She hadn't seen Drago, but he recognized her instantly as the woman who'd taken several shots at him a couple of years back in Tombstone. And she had been friends with Flower. It would be natural for her to step in to help an old friend.

Drago put a hand on the doctor's chest and shoved him hard into the door, breaking the glass.

"You're real lucky a lady came along to lead me to your patient, Doc. You were as close to dead as you'll ever get this side of a pine box," Drago sneered as he stepped off the boardwalk. The two of them began to follow Nettie.

Nettie pushed open the door to her bungalow with one hand while balancing a basket of warm biscuits, sliced meat, hard-boiled eggs, and some tinned fruit in the other.

"Flower, I'm here. I hope you're hungry."

She no more got inside than Drago and Cloyd pushed past her, knocking her to the floor. Drago drew his gun, pointed it at her head, and whispered, "If you make a sound, it will be your last."

Nettie just nodded as she tried to crawl away from him. Here she was, once again face-to-face with the man who had killed Jack Colson, the man she had loved and was about to marry when she lived in Tombstone. An honest, hardworking man she figured to make a family with, maybe even buy up some land.

Drago whispered to Cloyd to keep a gun on Nettie; then he quietly pushed open the door to the bedroom. Flower was on the bed, awakened by the noises coming from the other room. She froze as she found herself staring down the barrel of her husband's gun.

"You are an awful sight, woman," Drago said. "Don't you know better than to go traipsin' around in the desert durin' a summer day?"

Flower tried to say something, but it caught in her throat at the sight of the man she'd grown to hate so bitterly.

"What've you been sayin' to folks, my dear, sweet wife? Blabbin' about the stage robbery? Tellin' everyone you know who did it?"

"N-no, Emmett, I swear. I ain't told no one. Just leave me be, and go on about your business. I can keep my mouth shut, honestly." Flower was shaking with fear, tears flowing down her cheeks, stinging her bright red skin and blistered lips.

"Oh, I know you say I can trust you, my sweet. But I just can't take any chances. Get outta that bed, pronto. You and your friend in the other room are goin' on a little trip. Now, move!" He cocked the Colt and jabbed it into her stomach.

Flower moved as fast as she could, considering the pain she was in. But that wasn't fast enough for Drago. He grabbed her by the shoulders and yanked her out of bed, then threw her to the floor. A scream caught in her throat. She was sobbing hysterically now, which only made him madder.

Cloyd stepped into the bedroom, saw Flower all blistered and burned, then turned to Drago and said, "We plannin' on takin' them both, or should I kill the other one?"

"They both go. Havin' to brace that doctor was bad enough; we can't leave any more evidence that we was here for some nosy sheriff to use against us. Go round up some horses for these two, and meet us out back."

"What are you plannin' on doin' with them?" Cloyd still had feelings for Flower, even though he felt a strange repulsion at her looking the way she did, with her face slathered in grease and her arms wrapped in gauze.

"Well, we sure as the devil can't just turn 'em loose, now, can we? They'd be hollerin' their lungs out the moment we let 'em go. But I got a place in mind ain't no one goin' to locate till their bones turn to dust. Now, go get them horses, and be quick about it."

Cloyd scurried out the back door to find some unattended horses to steal. With two robberies and several murders hanging over their heads, he figured a charge of stealing wouldn't make a lot of difference. He found two mares tied out behind a saloon and led them down the alley to the back of the house. He was holding the reins of all four horses when Drago came out, shoving Flower in front of him and half dragging Nettie, who was trying to kick him and bite the hand that was squeezing her arm so tightly that the flow of blood was nearly cut off. He had gagged both of them with pieces of cloth ripped from the bedsheet so they couldn't cry out an alarm.

"You'll never get away with this, you pig," Nettie mumbled through the cloth wrapped around her mouth. Drago just laughed at her attempts to free herself from the ropes that now secured her to the saddle horn of one the stolen mares. He reveled in her futile struggle and enjoyed her discomfort. As he and Cloyd slowly led the ladies' horses down the alley between some vacant buildings at the end of the street and straight out into the desert, Nettie slumped in the saddle, aware that no one had seen them leave town. The chances of their ever being seen again alive dimmed with each step the horses took. She had no illusions as to her eventual fate, and she was saddened by the likelihood she would never see the young marshal again.

"Where to, Drago?" said Cloyd.

"Liberty. The old mine. Where else?"

Chapter Twenty-seven

It was getting dark, and Drago and Cloyd had yet to return to Liberty. Kelly was lost in thought as Sheriff Stevens burst through the door.

"The money came from both robberies, just like you figured, Marshal. But half the take from the first one is missing. You suppose they took it with them, and they ain't comin' back?"

"I think that's the money that Alvord had with him," said Kelly. "And now I'm concerned about something else. Assuming Drago already knew all about the robbery and had no need to actually go out to look over where the holdup took place, then he had some other reason to tear outta here like he'd just seen a rattler."

"What reason would that be?" Stevens settled into a rickety chair across from the marshal, who had just finished going through all of Drago's desk drawers. A wrinkled piece of paper sat in the middle of the desk.

"There is only one person who can identify him as one of the robbers. That's the woman who was on the stage. What if he just found out there was someone inside the coach? That could explain his strange behavior, his suddenly decidin' me and the Indian needed lockin' up."

"So, you figure he's gone to find her? And do what, maybe kill her?"

"A man like Drago may not figure he has any other choice. We have to get to her first."

"Well, the last time I saw her, she was at the Garcias' place. Might still be there," said Stevens.

"Then, that's where we'll start."

"Where are you taking us, you filthy animal?" said Nettie, after Drago had allowed Cloyd to remove the gags from his two prisoners.

"Don't make no difference where, woman. You ain't comin' back." Drago was clearly pleased at having eliminated possible testimony from the only two people who knew, or might know, that he and his deputy were robbers and murderers. He was even beginning to piece together a plan that could see him back in Liberty for a while, still serving as sheriff, with none of the townsfolk any the wiser. They would all be sympathetic to his story that his wife had been killed in an accident of some sort, maybe feel sorry enough to toss in a few free meals over at the hotel.

"They'll catch you and hang you like they should have in Tombstone when you gunned down Jack Colson," said Nettie. "Couldn't even face him, could you? Had to shoot him in the back."

Drago was beginning to bristle at the constant harassing he was getting from Nettie, a woman he'd as soon have shot on sight if circumstances had been different. Her beauty would have been no deterrent, either, for his lack of patience with women who didn't know their place was a powerful incentive to do them harm.

Seeing that his partner in crime was seething with anger—a time when mistakes got made—Cloyd decided it was time to speak up. "Drago, how 'bout you let me teach this mouthy one a lesson?"

"Yeah, sure, Cloyd. Just don't kill her yet, because we don't want to leave evidence of a fresh grave out here where someone might stumble across it. And I don't want to be haulin' a corpse around in this heat. Just rough her up a bit."

Cloyd took the reins of Nettie's horse and hung back from Drago and Flower. He had no intention of beating up a beautiful woman. He had other things on his mind. In fact, since he'd had no luck winning Flower's affection, maybe this one would be more reasonable.

"Look, ma'am, sayin' them things to Drago is just goin' to get you hurt—bad. Now, if you was to be appreciative, I think I might be able to keep you safe, maybe even get you outta this alive. What do you say? You gotta admit it's somethin' to think on."

The disgust Nettie felt for this pathetic little man rose

in her throat like bile. The very thought of his getting any closer than ten feet away made her stomach churn. She looked aside, trying to hold her contempt at bay until she could come up with a plan to get free on her own, without any help from this miserable excuse for a lawman.

Anticipating her response, Cloyd patiently rode alongside her, holding on to the hope that she might indeed see the logic in his offer. He wouldn't push her to make a decision, but then, he wasn't going to wait forever, either.

"I don't make deals with men who tie me up. Set me free—then we'll talk." The thought was enough to make her sick, but if tossing Cloyd a crumb could help her and Flower, then it was worth a try.

Cloyd was pleased that she hadn't rejected him outright like Flower had. He knew he couldn't cut Nettie loose without Drago's killing them both right on the spot, so he decided to be patient a little longer, maybe figure a way to get what he wanted and still keep the sheriff from exploding in a fit of anger and a hail of gunfire. And, while he hoped for some positive sign that the lady might favor him over death, he was going to have to be careful not to be in the middle if and when the shooting started.

Kelly decided to talk to the stationmaster before riding to the Garcia ranch. He wanted to find out what he could about the woman who was aboard in an attempt to discover why Drago apparently didn't know she was there.

"What can you tell me about the lady who took the stage to Cochise day before yesterday?" he asked. His boots echoed on the wood floor as he approached the thin-lipped man sitting at a paper-strewn desk behind the counter. A long bench along one wall served as the room's only other furniture, except for a large wall clock. Schedules of arrivals and departures were tacked to the wall next to the door. A placard leaned against a small fire bucket full of sand on the counter, enumerating the rules and regulations set by the stage line as to the expected behavior of all its passengers. *No spitting, no cursing, and always let a lady board first,* demanded the faded writing, almost as if a finger were pointed directly at anyone purchasing a ticket.

"Sorry, mister, there was no woman aboard the stage."

"You mean the coach pulled out of here empty?"

"Yes, sir."

"Then how could there have been a passenger?"

"Only way anyone could have been on that stage was if they met it outside of town after it left here."

Kelly started to leave, then, as an afterthought, said, "Did anyone buy a ticket recently who had yet to use it?"

"Just Miz Flower. She come in here a day or so before and bought a ticket. But she hadn't decided when she was goin'."

"What does this 'Flower' look like?"

"Pretty woman—blond, slim, fancy-like. Reckon that's why the sheriff married her in the first place."

"Flower is Sheriff Drago's wife?"

"Sure as you're standin' there askin' fool questions, Marshal. Say, what's th—"

The stationmaster didn't get a chance to finish his sentence before Kelly slammed through the door at a dead run toward Stevens and Spotted Dog, where they waited outside the sheriff's office.

"What'd the stationmaster have to say?" asked Stevens.

"The woman we found in the road fits the description of Drago's wife. He probably had no idea she was on that stagecoach, since it pulled out of town empty, and therefore he never looked inside. But by now he probably knows. And if he finds her before we do, she's more'n likely a dead woman."

Stevens and Spotted Dog were mounted before Kelly finished untying his gelding. The three of them kicked their mounts to a run, straight out of town toward the relay station, with a prayer that they could reach Flower Drago before her desperate husband did.

Part of Nettie's plan was to try as hard as she could to keep her mouth shut. Maybe that way Cloyd would think she was still considering his proposition. But as they got closer and closer to Liberty, she knew she'd have to come up with something better than a "maybe." If she could attract the attention of one of the locals when they arrived in town, she might have a chance to escape or, better yet, get word to Marshal Kelly of her predicament.

But her heart sank at the next words she heard. Drago wasn't fool enough to let anyone see either her or Flower. Their fate was fast becoming hopeless as Drago left the road several miles outside of town and headed across the desert.

"We goin' straight for the mine, Sheriff?" said Cloyd.

"That's right. We'll shoot these two, bury 'em at the mine, then go to town to see what has transpired. Maybe we'll start the townsfolk thinkin' about a little necktie party for them two we got locked up. We can claim we found out for sure they were the killers. Folks'll get so riled, they'll just naturally want to string 'em up. We wouldn't want to stand in the way of justice, now, would we?" Drago laughed at the idea of waltzing right into town and getting off free as the wind with all that loot and no one the wiser.

"That's a good plan, Sheriff. But I thought we were gonna split the money and head out for New Mexico or California." Cloyd was upset with Drago's newly announced strategy. He thought they were already taking too many chances by grabbing two women out of a strange town and dragging them clear across the desert, then killing them. Cloyd could see the charges piling up faster than he could count if they got caught. He could almost feel the rope tightening around his scrawny neck. It made a lump form in his throat.

"I just figured that, since these two didn't get a chance to tell anybody about us, why not go back to livin' our lives as before—of course, without Flower constantly on my back, stranglin' the life outta me. I been givin' it some thought, and I can't keep her alive, 'cause, sure as shootin', she'd blab to somebody. She never could keep her mouth shut—always blabbin' about somethin' or other. We'll wait in Liberty until the trail gets too cold for anyone to hunt for us, then we'll light out for the hinterlands and spend our money as we wish."

Cloyd needed to think this over. He'd had too much experience with Drago's constantly changing all the rules, a situation he had grown tired of. Also, he didn't like the idea of having to kill Nettie, especially if there was any chance she might go off with him, be his girl. He needed to figure a way to get his share of the money and keep Nettie safe, all to himself. And, of course, not get himself shot down in the process.

"Do you think we can convince the town that the ones that done the killin' was that tall, stringy fellow with the mustache and his old Indian friend?"

Nettie was stung by hearing those words. She blurted out, "Well, Drago, looks like you've done it now. You truly are a fool. Do you have any idea who that 'tall fella' is? He's Piedmont Kelly, a United States Marshal, that's who. And when he catches up to you, he'll nail your hide to the barn. You're a dead man, Drago, and it couldn't happen to a more deserving skunk."

Nettie's words slapped at Drago like a bullwhip. Panic flooded his senses. If what Nettie said was true, he would have to change his plans—but only the part about returning to Liberty, not the part about shooting two mouthy women. That part wasn't about to change. Not if he could help it.

Cloyd, too, felt a shiver go up his back at Nettie's

proclamation. His confusion as to what he should do was overcoming his ability to sort everything out. His inclination to end it all by gunning down Drago while his back was turned was fast becoming uppermost in the deputy's mind, flooding out any possibility of a logical solution. His hand slowly moved toward his Colt.

Chapter Twenty-eight

Kelly held up a hand at the sight of someone riding hard toward them, raising a terrific amount of dust. It was Sam Arrowsmith, one of the men Sheriff Stevens had hastily chosen for his posse when the stage was late getting into Cochise, then later sent to the Garcia place with Flower Drago.

"I figured I'd find you out this way, Sheriff. I got some bad news. That woman we found in the road and took to the relay station was brought into town by Antonio Garcia for the doc to look after. Well, she apparently left Doc Reynolds' place and was grabbed by a couple of rough-looking hombres. They stole a couple of horses on their way out of town too. And what's worse, it looks like they kidnapped Nettie too."

The shock of hearing that Nettie was in potential danger hit Kelly hard. *She had nothing to do with all this. Why kidnap her?* He sat stunned for several seconds before speaking.

"Why do you figure they took Nettie, Sam?"

"Doc Reynolds says it's likely 'cause she was the only one who wanted to help the woman. She visited some and brought her food. Doc figures the lady was there with Nettie when the men broke into her house."

"*Her* house? Why was the woman at Nettie's house?"

"Doc figures it's 'cause Nettie might have been thinkin' to hide the lady out from someone who was after her. He said he overheard them talkin' and thought they had been close from some other time. Leastways, that was the impression he got."

How did Nettie even know the wife of Sheriff Emmett Drago?

"Did anyone get a good look at the two men?"

"Bartender said they was rough-lookin'. One was a short, dirty little man, and the other, taller, gruff, kinda sour-lookin', wearin' a bowler."

"Sure sounds like Drago and Cloyd," Kelly muttered.

Where there had been no real plan before, one began to form in the marshal's mind. He knew he had to act fast if he were to save both women from a man who had shown no reluctance to kill when it served him. A man whose actions of late seemed always to point to the same goal: to allow himself to do whatever served his purpose, unencumbered by propriety, morality, or the law.

"What've you a mind to do now?" said Sheriff Stevens.

Kelly ignored Stevens' question as he again turned to Sam. "Do you have any idea which direction they took?"

"Well, at first tracks seemed to lead toward Liberty, but then they broke off 'bout four miles back, took off through the desert, out thataway," Sam said, pointing toward the Chiricahua range.

Stevens spoke up at hearing that. "That's about the same direction as those tracks I followed to that old mine. You suppose that's where they're headed, still usin' the same method to elude trackers?"

"Makes sense they'd go for their loot before gettin' rid of the two ladies," said Kelly. "But if we're wrong, lives could be at stake. We'll split up. I'll go back to Liberty first, then backtrack to the mine. You and Spotted Dog follow those tracks and make sure they're goin' where we figure, John Henry."

"Okay. Sam, we'll ride back a ways to where they broke off the trail. Then, if you got the time, I'd be obliged if you could come along. I could use the manpower."

Sam nodded his willingness to help out again. John Henry was visibly relieved to have someone along other than an old Indian he had yet to warm up to.

Kelly wheeled his gelding around, dug his heels into the horse's flanks, and urged him into a gallop. The others headed back westward to pick up the outlaws' tracks leading out into the desert.

As much as he wanted to see Drago and Cloyd pay for their crimes, Kelly was even more concerned about Nettie's welfare. He felt a strange mixture of anxiety and something else he couldn't explain. But he knew he couldn't get her out of his mind and hadn't been able to for days.

He pushed his mount even harder as he could see time becoming an enemy, one that favored the outlaws.

Spotted Dog was in the lead most of the time as the three men slowly backtracked the route supposedly taken by the two outlaws and their female captives. It wasn't exactly the same as that Stevens had followed from the scene of the stage robbery. But the efforts taken by the outlaws to elude capture followed the same pattern—changing direction frequently, leaving false trails, then backtracking to a different course, all designed to make the job of any posse that much more difficult. Clearly, Drago knew a thing or two about how to elude a stalker.

Reaching the top of a rocky hillock, they stopped to survey the valley below, in hopes of spotting their prey. Sheriff Stevens sat for several minutes, staring at the open expanse and saying nothing. Finally he turned to Sam and asked, "You see anything of them?"

"Just cactus, mesquite, and sand. Not a darned thing else. You figure they're sittin' out there laughing at us?"

"Probably so. I reckon we better push on, anyway. Won't find 'em sittin' here gawkin' at the scenery. Spotted Dog, how about you continue takin' the lead? You're about our only chance to find them varmints before they get to where they're goin' and find out they been robbed."

When the old Indian didn't push his mount to the front of the others, Stevens turned around to suggest he listen to orders, but Spotted Dog was nowhere to be seen.

"Spotted Dog, can you hear me?"

No sound reached their ears other than that of an occasional breeze rustling some nearby brittlebush and a roadrunner that darted across in front of them, its head feathers laid back to protect its dark skin from the sun.

"Now, just where did that Apache slip off to? Did you see him leave, Sam?"

"I ain't laid eyes on him for several minutes, Sheriff. I figured you'd sent him out to scout another direction or somethin'."

"Well, I didn't, and if he's gone, we're in a real pickle. 'Cause I don't have any idea where we are, nor how to get to wherever it is we got to go. I'll tell you this, I could easily grow to dislike Injuns."

Sam stood up in his stirrups, one hand shading his eyes, and said, "I think Liberty is over in that direction. Maybe we should just go there."

"Hmm. That ain't what the marshal wanted us to do, but if that's our only way of finding civilization, I say we get to it. Otherwise we could wander around out here till winter."

The two of them headed off and hoped for the best, since neither knew this part of the Territory.

"Well, ladies, the time of your demise is gettin' close. Can you feel it? Death seems to fill your nostrils out here where critters feed on one another, natural-like, every day. But don't neither of you worry—it'll be quick and painless . . . mostly." Drago roared with laughter.

He was getting great joy out of his revenge on Flower for putting him into this predicament. At least, that's the way he saw it. It was all her fault. If she hadn't been on that stagecoach, no one would have ever been the wiser about his and Cloyd's involvement in theft and murder. He intended that she clearly understood it was her fault. All of it.

"You may kill us, Drago," Nettie said, "but you'll never escape that marshal. I hear he can put a bullet clean through a silver dollar at two hundred yards. When he finds you, he'll explode that evil heart of yours with one shot. You'll never spend one nickel of the loot you killed to get." Nettie's voice oozed bitter contempt for the man who'd shot down someone she loved. Of course, she'd made up that part about Kelly's extraordinary skills with his Winchester. But what would it hurt if it put even an ounce of fear into Drago's cold heart?

Watching him and hearing the hatred he had for Flower, she had come to the sad realization that she *was* going to die, Cloyd's feeble attempt to win her affections notwithstanding. She understood Drago, or at least the type of man he was. A desperate, evil outlaw without respect for life or anything good and honest. He had to get rid of anyone who could put him squarely in the middle of his murders. *And Cloyd, that filthy, miserable weakling, can do nothing to stop him.*

Flower kneed her horse closer to Nettie's. Drago and Cloyd seemed—for the moment, at least—to be ignoring the women, probably lost in their plans for where they'd go after retrieving their ill-gotten gains.

"I was able to snag my little handbag before Drago dragged me outta your house, Nettie, but I can't get my hands free to get inside. I put a derringer in there. If I could get to it, maybe I could at least get one shot at that miserable snake," Flower whispered.

"I can't even feel my hands anymore, these ropes are so tight. It doesn't look good for any chance of escape," Nettie whispered back in a voice so filled with despair that Flower could hardly hear her. Her heart sank at the prospect of never seeing the marshal again.

When Kelly reached Liberty, he grabbed his rifle and rushed into the sheriff's office. Deakins was still inside.

When he saw the marshal, he stood up. "Marshal, I found this paper in the desk. It says Cloyd is wanted for rustlin'. I don't understand how Drago could have hired him, knowin' he was a wanted man."

"I'm afraid you're in for even more disturbin' news. Drago and Cloyd have kidnapped two women from Cochise. It looks like they're the ones who killed the stage driver and the guard. Have you seen them since we left here?"

"No, I ain't seen hide nor hair of either of 'em. You sayin' they are murd—"

Before Deakins could finish his sentence, Kelly bolted back through the doorway, mounted his horse, and urged the big gelding to a full run as he headed for the mine. It was getting late, and the afternoon sun cast long shadows from the buildings, like dark spires lying across the roadway. Several people scampered for the boardwalk as the marshal drove his horse hard down the dusty street with little regard for pedestrians. His nerves were taut, and the sound of pounding hooves was his only comfort, giving him a meager hope that he might reach the mine in time to save two innocent lives and capture—or kill—the worst kind of filth: men who would pervert the law they had sworn to uphold.

He swung his horse off the road and down into a draw with a small creek running through it in hopes of saving some time. But as he splashed across the creek and up the other side, he heard a sound that sent a chill up his back. Gunshots, several of them in quick succession. Near panic gripped him as the dread of getting to the rise just in time to see Nettie and Flower Drago shot down overcame him. Drago and Cloyd would be in a fury over finding their loot missing.

But as he came upon the road at a point only about thirty feet from the mine entrance, he saw two still forms standing under a cottonwood tree, almost as if in a trance. He dismounted before his gelding had come to a stop, jumping down in a swirl of dust and a crunch of gravel, and ran to them.

Nettie and Flower stood frozen at the sight that lay before them, hands still bound. As Kelly ran up, rifle in hand, Nettie turned to him. Flower remained where she was, shaking her head, tears running down her cheeks.

At the entrance to the mine, Drago and Cloyd lay in the dirt, dead. They had each been shot several times.

Kelly couldn't believe his eyes. He looked around for whoever had done this but saw no one. And, unable to tell him anything more than that the shots came from behind some trees and that she'd not seen a soul, Nettie just clung to him, shaking like a frightened kitten, her chest heaving as she sobbed. He held her close, knowing that answers would come soon enough.

Chapter Twenty-nine

After briefly searching the area for where the shots had likely come from and finding nothing, Kelly began hefting the two dead men across their saddles and securing them with their own ropes. He then took their horses' reins in one hand to lead the procession back to Liberty. Still dazed by the events of the past few hours, Flower and Nettie followed on the two horses stolen from Cochise. As the threesome reached the town limits, a crowd began to gather and follow them down the street. People began gathering in front of the jail as the marshal and the ladies dismounted. Sheriff Stevens and Sam Arrowsmith had arrived minutes before.

"What happened, Kelly?" said Stevens. "How'd you get the drop on them two?"

"I didn't. But somebody sure did, and I'd say they

did a fair job of it too. I doubt these two even saw it comin'. Their sidearms were still in their holsters."

"Drago was good with a six-gun. I'm surprised someone got that close," said Stevens, shaking his head at the sight.

"Don't have to get close with rifles. I'd guess about five of them."

"Rifles? But who . . ."

"Where's Spotted Dog, John Henry?"

"I don't know. He lit out somewheres among the rocks, leavin' us to fend for ourselves. Since we didn't know which way the mine was, and the tracks we were followin' had petered out, we thought to come on into town, in hopes of findin' you."

"Marshal, would it be all right if I took Flower inside and made her comfortable? She's been through a lot the last couple of days," said Nettie in an uncharacteristically quiet voice.

"Of course, I should have thought of that myself. Take her inside and let her lie down on one of the bunks in a cell." Kelly reached out to help them both.

"Marshal, what happened out there? Who killed the sheriff and his deputy?" asked several voices all at once from those gathered about.

"Your sheriff and his deputy were responsible for two stagecoach robberies and at least six, probably seven, murders. They were about to add these two ladies to their score. Thankfully, someone got to them before they could kill any more innocent people."

The crowd began to get restless as several men expressed doubts as to the veracity of such a statement.

"How do you know they done the killings, Marshal? Drago was a good sheriff, and he seemed to be a good man. Why, he had a wife and was all settled down in his own house, which the town paid for, and he was a fine citizen from all appearances. That's his woman that rode in with you," said a man who had pushed his way through from the back of the crowd.

Before Kelly could begin to explain the evidence that had led him to his conclusion, Flower reemerged from the door to the jail.

"Listen to the marshal. He's tellin' the truth. I was on that stage when my husband and that skunk he called a deputy held it up and shot two men down as if they were mongrel dogs. They did what the marshal said, all right, and they got what was comin' to them. This town will be better off without the likes of those two," she said, her anger slowly overcoming the fear that had gripped her for days.

Flower's speech brought the crowd to complete silence. Confused by the news, they began to disperse. One man turned, scratched his head, and said, "What're we gonna do for law now?"

"Well, it appears Deakins here was duly sworn in before Drago left town, so I'd say you've at least got yourself a deputy until you can elect a new sheriff," said Kelly.

The crowd now leaving, Kelly sent Sam to find the undertaker to handle the two bodies. "And when you're finished, take their horses to the stable. Deakins can sell 'em and give the money from Drago's horse to his wife. Cloyd's can go to the town, unless someone knows of any next of kin."

Inside, Stevens was clearly baffled by the turn of events. He leaned against a wall, staring out the front window and chewing on his lower lip. Flower had reclined on one of the two bunks in the back, and Nettie was seated in the desk chair. She, too, looked puzzled, as well as weary and worn down from her ordeal.

"Nettie, how do you suppose Drago knew Flower was at your place?" said Kelly, unable to close the books on recent happenings without all the answers.

"Probably recognized me when I left the restaurant. You see, I knew him from before," she said, staring at the desktop, unable or unwilling to meet his eyes. "And Flower and me, we were old friends too."

"When we first met, you said your husband had been killed in Tombstone. I recall you started to say his name was Col-something, but then you changed your mind about both the name and the location. Care to explain?"

"I, uh, suppose I didn't want to admit certain things to you, Marshal. There's some of my past I'm not all that proud of."

"We all make mistakes, Nettie. I'm sure yours are no worse than most, mine included."

"I'll bet you never shot a man in the back like he was of no worth at all."

"No, I haven't."

"That's what that rattlesnake Emmett Drago did to Jack Colson, the man I was going to marry."

"Why didn't the law take Drago in?" said Kelly.

"He *was* the law, that's why. Drago was a deputy for Marshal Fred White before Curley Bill Brocius shot White down. Oh, White fired Drago for what he did, but there was no trial, no punishment. He never served one minute for back-shooting an innocent man," said Nettie, her eyes filling with tears.

"Why did Drago go after Colson?"

Nettie hung her head. "Do you really have to know?"

"I think it might go a long way toward explainin' some things that have happened, if you can bring yourself to tell me."

Nettie sank deeper into the chair, then clasped her hands on the desk in front of her and began in a near whisper, as if the very hearing of her confession would turn him from her forever.

"Flower and I worked in one of the town's saloons. Drago had expressed a particular interest in me. The sight of him and the thought of his touching me turned my stomach, and I told him as much. He then turned his attention to Flower, a vulnerable girl with no experience handling toughs like him. When he saw that I favored a cowboy named Colson, Drago did everything he could to provoke a fight, to get Colson to draw first. When that didn't work, Drago found a wanted dodger with a likeness that resembled Jack, so he confronted him. Jack denied being wanted for anything, but Drago said he was going to jail, anyway, until he could prove he wasn't wanted. When they took the argument out into the street, Drago pulled his Colt and shot Jack in the back, claiming he'd tried to run."

"What was it Colson was supposedly wanted for?"

"I never knew. I left Tombstone soon afterward, took what money I'd saved, and came to Cochise for a fresh start."

"I reckon I can understand your distrust of lawmen. I'm sorry you've only seen those that have chosen to ride both sides of the fence."

"Now that you know the truth about me, maybe we could start over, fresh?"

"I'd like that, Nettie. There's nothin' better than the truth to cement a friendship."

"I've got some questions of my own, Piedmont," said Stevens. "Like who in tarnation gunned down them two skunks?"

"Why, John Henry, I thought you'd have that figured out by now. Spotted Dog and his four Apache scout friends did it to avenge the killing of the Indians where Spotted Dog was shot and left for dead."

"Hmm. I can see how that makes sense. But what was it that put you on to Drago's bein' involved in the first place?"

"Tracks. When I saw that Alvord's horse's tracks were beneath the tracks of the Indians, I knew that Alvord and whoever he was riding with had reached that clearing and the cave first. They probably were surprised by the Indians' arrival and saw them as an impediment to their escape after dividing the money from the first stage robbery."

"So they just sat up there and gunned them down, huh?"

"That's right. If Drago hadn't said he and his deputy had tracked five Indians after the holdup and killed all but one in a battle, I might never have put him with Alvord. But when I found out they were friends, it made sense that Drago was involved."

"Now that we got all the money from the second robbery and half of it from the first, I reckon we could set out for Cochise in the mornin', huh, Marshal?" said Stevens. "I'm saddle sore and in need of a real bed before my back plumb gives out on me."

"I could go for some of that home cookin' over at Nettie's too," said Kelly, turning his eyes to her, which seemed instantly to raise her spirits.

"We could maybe leave early in the morning and be in Cochise by late afternoon," said Stevens. "Flower said she can't face staying in Liberty another day."

"Then we'll get the ladies a hotel room, and we three can bunk here in the jail tonight," said Kelly.

The next morning, as all five were preparing to leave Liberty, Flower insisted she had something important to do before she could go. Nettie asked if there was any way she could help, but Flower refused any assistance, insisting it was personal and that she'd be back in a few minutes.

Kelly went to the bank to leave instructions as to the disposition of the stolen money he and Stevens had left with them for safekeeping. "Someone from the stage company will be in touch before long. Just be sure they show you proper credentials before you release the money. It's had too many hands on it already," said Kelly. The bank manager smiled at the implication as the marshal strolled out and headed back to the others awaiting him outside the jail.

The sky was clear, and the day promised to be extremely hot, as was common for late summer in the southeastern part of the Arizona Territory. Only a handful of wispy clouds hovered over the Chiricahua peaks far off in the distance. Knowing there would be no respite from the hot sun, Kelly had insisted they each carry two canteens of water. And at Nettie's insistence, Flower would be expected to make full use of one of the two umbrellas Nettie had purchased the very second the general store opened.

Flower finally reappeared, coming at a fast pace from between two buildings across the street. As soon as she was mounted, the group began their journey.

After they had gone no more than a quarter mile outside of town, Kelly turned and saw smoke billowing from a small cabin on a hill on the other side of Liberty.

"What do you suppose that is?" he mused aloud.

"You can call it my final revenge," Flower murmured. She just stared back at the cabin with a look of relief as it was quickly engulfed in flames.

Chapter Thirty

As the five tired, hot, and generally miserable riders straggled into Cochise at four o'clock in the afternoon, Stevens was the first to dismount, which he did with an audible groan and a few choice words about saddles, cacti, and other inconveniences of the past few days. He stomped across the boardwalk and into the jail, slapping trail dust from his britches as he went. He dropped into his swivel chair, pulled off his boots, leaned back, and put his feet on the desk with utter disregard for anyone paying attention to the multitude of holes in his socks or any potential odor.

"I'll be so thankful for a bath, a shave, some decent food, and a good night's sleep, I'd give everything I own to have it all and not have to move one inch from this chair to get it."

Nettie and Flower left immediately for Nettie's house.

Neither said a word but let it be known by their own moans and groans that they were seriously thinking of sitting in a soothing tub of hot water for the rest of the day.

Sam Arrowsmith went directly back to his business without mincing words as to his joy at having returned alive, and, though not wishing to be unappreciative, suggested he would rather not be considered for posse duty again anytime soon.

Kelly stood at the front window, staring out at the comings and goings of the citizenry as they went on with their lives, as if it mattered not a whit that within the past twenty-four hours two desperate men had been gunned down in a hail of bullets, their regrettable lives now just a footnote for local historians. He shifted from foot to foot, adjusted his gun belt, pulled his Colt, half cocked it and, rolling the cylinder through a couple of times, stuck it back into its holster, removed his Stetson, finger-combed his hair, then replaced the hat and began twisting the ends of his mustache. All this was clearly unnerving to Stevens, who, by now, would have settled in for a snooze were it not for Kelly's distracting activities.

"Consarn it, Marshal, can't you find a place to light? You're disruptin' my nap."

"Sorry, John Henry, I'm just tryin' to put the last part of this whole affair to rest."

"What's to put anywhere? Them two rattlers robbed, killed, and then got their comeuppance. And we recovered most of the money. That's that. It's time to put it to bed," said the sheriff, trying to stifle a yawn.

"Well, not quite. You put your finger on the problem: We recovered *most* of the money. There's still the question of the other half of the loot from the first robbery. Who was the fourth member of the Drago bunch? And who killed George Alvord?"

Stevens sat up straight, no longer sleepy as he, too, began to ponder those serious questions.

"I reckon I'd completely forgotten that fourth person. Got any ideas?" While Kelly continued to ponder the question, the sheriff got up, stretched, then went into the back where the cells were to grab a blanket off one of the bunks.

"What are you doing, John Henry?"

"The thought just came to me to get these blankets washed from when your Indian friend slept on 'em. Got a little blood on this one."

Kelly went back to staring out the front window as he mumbled something about someone's having said Alvord had a cousin in Cochise and wondering how he'd locate him, just as Stevens came back into the office.

"You know that old Apache got blood all over the floor in the back cell too. I should have made *him* clean it up," said Stevens, pulling a face.

"What? Spotted Dog was never *in* the back cell. Let's take a look," said Kelly.

Kelly pushed past Stevens, whose mouth fell open in a puzzled expression. The marshal flung open the unlocked door to the back cell. There were several splotches of dried blood beneath the bunk near the wall. He bent down to look closer.

"John Henry, bring me somethin' to pry up this floor-board. It's loose. In fact, it looks as if it's been taken up recently."

The sheriff squatted beside the marshal, handing him a pocketknife. Kelly inserted the point between two boards and pried one of them upward so he could get a grip on it. It came out easily once leverage was applied. There, in a space beneath the floor, sat the saddlebags Alvord had been carrying when he came into Kelly's camp. Between the splotches of dried blood on the floor and the bulging saddlebags, all Kelly's questions had suddenly been answered.

"Whoever stashed this here was bleedin' at the time. Where's Jed, John Henry?"

"I don't know. In fact, I haven't seen Jed since we got back. I'll go check at the saloon."

"Where does he keep his horse? Does he have a room in town?"

"He lives in a shanty out behind the Gold Mine Saloon, across the alley. Keeps his horse in a corral beside it. Say, why the sudden interest in Jed?"

Kelly ignored the question and left the door standing open as he trotted across the street, then down the alley behind the saloon. When he reached a ramshackle structure, it was clear no one was inside. The door was open, and the corral was empty. He headed for the saloon and entered through a back door. John Henry was questioning the bartender.

"So, you say Jed left about an hour ago?"

"Yep. When he got sight of you and the marshal

bringin' them ladies back to town, he lit outta here like a scared rabbit. All he said was, 'I'll be hornswoggled.' "

"Did you see which direction he was headed in?" said Kelly.

"It sorta sounded like he was headin' north," said the bartender.

As Kelly and Stevens went back to the jail, the sheriff said, "Sounds like you figure that Jed was the fourth gunman. That what's got you all riled?"

"It adds up. Folks in Liberty said Alvord had a cousin livin' here in Cochise, although they didn't know his name. Jed carried a bowie knife, and it was a large blade that was used to kill Alvord. I shot and wounded the man that night, and you said Jed had a recent gunshot wound. He also recognized the Indian when I brought him in. I'll bet he remembered him from when he and the rest of the gang ambushed the Apaches. And the blood on the jail floor is probably Jed's. Who else could have hidden the loot there? Unless *you're* ready to confess to being part of Drago's bunch, I'd say Jed fits the bill." Kelly looked Stevens squarely in the eye, awaiting a response.

"I-I'm afraid you're right. It seems to add up," said Stevens. "I reckon we better get saddled up again and go after him."

Kelly was already retrieving his horse as Stevens shuffled after him, too dog-tired to be starting another chase but clearly seeing the need to let no more time pass to allow the deputy a clean getaway.

"You stay here, John Henry. I'll track him myself. You need some rest. It wouldn't hurt none if you were to look in on the ladies, though," Kelly said, already in the saddle, Winchester in hand. He slapped the reins and urged the gelding to a run, heading into the mountains north of town.

Less than a mile outside of town the ground rose quickly into foothills littered with large boulders, and he reined in the gelding among them behind a thick growth of mesquite and paloverde. He pulled his field glass from a saddlebag. And waited.

The sun was beginning to play hide-and-seek with the mountains to the west, and shadows spread across the town like melting butter. That's when what Piedmont Kelly was expecting to see happen began to take shape. As he watched the front of the jail through the glass, he saw a dark figure slowly emerge from the alley behind the jail and, keeping well in the shadows, slip in through the front door, gun drawn. It was obvious whoever it was had no intention of being seen. It was time for the marshal to make his move.

When Kelly got back to the jail, he stopped before stepping up onto the boardwalk, hoping to surprise the man he was now certain had been an accomplice in several murders. As he eased closer to the door, he heard the sounds of things and curses being tossed about liberally by the irate deputy.

"Damn you, old man!" shouted Jed. "What did you do with my money?"

But Kelly heard no reply. He froze. Had his leaving town, even briefly, made the sheriff a target? Kelly eased along the front wall and slipped unheard through the open door.

The deputy had his back to the marshal. He was bent over behind the desk, yanking out drawers and dumping them upside down.

Kelly shouted, "You're under arrest, Jed. It's over!"

Shocked at the words, Jed stood up, spun around suddenly, and found himself facing the business end of a Winchester rifle no more than two feet from his head. He started to go for his revolver, then hesitated, realizing he'd have no chance. He threw up his hands. "Don't shoot, Marshal. I give up," the deputy said with a tone of defeat.

From a corner of the room Kelly heard a moan and saw John Henry slowly getting to his feet, rubbing the side of his head where a splotch of blood spread across his cheek and ran down onto his shirt. Kelly disarmed Jed and herded him into the first cell, then locked the door. He went back out to check on the condition of the sheriff.

"I'll be all right—just gonna have a fierce headache for a spell. He caught me off guard," said Stevens. "I didn't even hear him come in. I only remember gettin' hit with somethin', probably the butt of a pistol. Reckon there's no doubt about him bein' in on the first robbery now. Probably took part in killin' them Indians too, like you said."

Kelly just nodded as he returned to the cell where Jed sat on the edge of the bunk, his head hung down.

"Why'd you sneak up on Alvord and murder him in his sleep?"

"My dear cousin was runnin' out on me. He slammed me in the head with his rifle and left me in the desert to die. But I didn't, did I? Lucky for me his horse had a bad shoe, or I'd likely never been able to track him."

"I reckon my shot *did* find its mark when you tried to get me too. But why'd you come back here? Why not light out for Liberty and your friends?"

"They'd've killed me for sure when they found out George was dead and I had his share too. I had to stay as far away as possible from Liberty. I come back here to get patched up by the doc. I told the sheriff I shot myself accidentally, and I hid the money in the back cell. I figured this was as safe a place as any until things cooled off."

"So you have no remorse for killin' your own cousin?"

"He deserved what he got."

"Did those Apaches you ambushed deserve what they got too?" said Kelly, bitterness in his tone.

"They was Injuns, wasn't they?" mumbled Jed.

"You would have been better off if you'd never thrown in with men like Alvord and Drago. Now all you have to look forward to is stretching a rope."

Kelly turned away in disgust from the sight of the degenerate deputy whose disregard for life and unbridled greed had left him with no future. The marshal went outside, looking for a breath of fresh air and a place to lay his head for the night.

Sometime around midnight, while he was snoring loudly in the back cell, Sheriff Stevens was suddenly awakened by a yell that nearly curdled his blood. Not fully awake, he jumped up and stumbled over his own boots, trying to shake off the sleep as he struggled to get up and investigate. As he ran out front, still wriggling into his suspenders and gripping a shotgun hastily retrieved from the gun rack, he looked around anxiously but found the street empty, all except for Alvord's horse, which had been tied to the hitching rail out front.

Spotted Dog had returned the property that didn't belong to him. Two hawk feathers were woven into the mane near the horse's ears, a mark of respect for an animal that had served the Indian well.

Kelly spent the next week in Cochise, resting up, eating regular meals, and getting much better acquainted with Nettie. As he placed his bedroll behind the cantle and secured it with saddle strings, Nettie stood with her arms crossed, looking wistful.

"I hate to leave, but there's been some trouble around Bisbee," Kelly said.

"Will you be coming back this way?" she asked cautiously.

"Wild horses couldn't keep me away," he said as he reached over to run his fingers through her hair. She flung her arms around him and kissed him hard. He returned the gesture, pulling her close. When they parted, he swung easily into the saddle, touched the brim of his Stetson, and gave her a wink. He nudged his gelding to a slow walk.

As he passed the jail, Sheriff Stevens was on the

porch in a rocker he'd dragged outside. He squinted as the marshal approached.

"You look like you got somethin' on your mind, John Henry. Better spit it out," said Kelly.

"I was just wonderin' how you'll look all twisted up in apron strings," Stevens said with a broad smile. "Purty, I'll bet. Real purty."